Main

PHILIP ALLAN
LITERATURE GUIDE
FOR A-LEVEL

A STREETCAR NAMED DESIRE
TENNESSEE WILLIAMS

Nicola Onyett

PHILIP ALLAN
UPDATES

Philip Allan Updates, an imprint of Hodder Education, an Hachette UK company, Market Place, Deddington, Oxfordshire OX15 0SE

Orders

Bookpoint Ltd, 130 Milton Park, Abingdon, Oxfordshire OX14 4SB
tel: 01235 827827
fax: 01235 400401
e-mail: education@bookpoint.co.uk

Lines are open 9.00 a.m.–5.00 p.m., Monday to Saturday, with a 24-hour message answering service. You can also order through the Philip Allan Updates website: www.philipallan.co.uk

© Nicola Onyett 2011

ISBN 978-1-4441-2156-8

First printed 2011

Impression number 5 4 3

Year 2015 2014 2013 2012

Printed in Spain

Hachette UK's policy is to use papers that are natural, renewable and recyclable products and made from wood grown in sustainable forests. The logging and manufacturing processes are expected to conform to the environmental regulations of the country of origin.

Cover photo: Marlon Brando as Stanley Kowalski in the 1951 film version of _A Streetcar Named Desire._ © SNAP/Rex Features

Contents

Using this guide

Why read this guide?

The purposes of this A-level Literature Guide are to enable you to organise your thoughts and responses to the text, deepen your understanding of key features and aspects and help you to address the particular requirements of examination questions and coursework tasks in order to obtain the best possible grade. It will also prove useful to those of you writing a coursework piece on the text as it provides a number of summaries, lists, analyses and references to help with the content and construction of the assignment.

Note that teachers and examiners are seeking above all else evidence of an *informed personal response to the text*. A guide such as this can help you to understand the text, form your own opinions, and suggest areas to think about, but it cannot replace your own ideas and responses as an informed and autonomous reader.

Page references in this guide refer to the Methuen student edition of *A Streetcar Named Desire* edited by Patricia Hern and Michael Hooper (2009). This edition has excellent introductory material and comprehensive notes. Where a publication is given in the 'Taking it further' section on pp. 92–93, the author's surname and publication date only are cited after the first full reference.

How to make the most of this guide

You may find it useful to read sections of this guide when you need them, rather than reading it from start to finish. For example, you may find it helpful to read the *Contexts* section before you start reading the text, or to read the *Scene summaries and commentaries* section in conjunction with the text — whether to back up your first reading of it at school or college or to help you revise. The sections relating to the Assessment Objectives will be especially useful in the weeks leading up to the exam.

Key elements

Look at the Context boxes to find interesting facts that are relevant to the text.

Context

Be exam-ready

Broaden your thinking about the text by answering the questions in the **Pause for Thought** boxes. These help you to consider your own opinions in order to develop your skills of criticism and analysis.

*Pause for **Thought*** ❙❙

Build critical skills

Taking it Further boxes suggest poems, films, etc. that provide further background or illuminating parallels to the text.

Taking it **Further** ➤

Where to find out more

Use the Task boxes to develop your understanding of the text and test your knowledge of it. Answers for some of the tasks are given online, and do not forget to look online for further self-tests on the text.

Task

Test yourself

A cross-reference to a **Top ten quotation** (see pages 89–92 of this guide), where each quotation is accompanied by a commentary that shows why it is important.

❮ Top ten *quotation*

Know your text

Don't forget to go online: **www.philipallan.co.uk/literatureguidesonline** where you can find masses of additional resources **free**, including interactive questions, podcasts, exam answers and a glossary.

Synopsis

Blanche DuBois, an English teacher from Laurel, Mississippi, arrives to stay with her sister and brother-in-law, Stella and Stanley Kowalski, in their cramped apartment in a lively multicultural working-class district of New Orleans. All is clearly not well; the sisters' childhood home, Belle Reve, has been mysteriously 'lost' and Blanche has left her job because of her bad nerves.

Blanche proves a troublesome guest; she hogs the bathroom, expects the pregnant Stella to fetch and carry for her and drinks Stanley's whisky on the sly even while criticising the Kowalskis' 'common' way of life. At first Stanley suspects Blanche has cheated Stella out of her share of the family inheritance, but it becomes clear that Belle Reve was repossessed after the family defaulted on a mortgage.

One evening Stanley and his friends play poker and Mitch, who lives with his sick mother, is attracted to Blanche. An ugly scene erupts which ends with Stanley hitting his pregnant wife. Although Stella runs upstairs to take refuge with her friend Eunice, when Stanley calls for her she returns. Despite everything, they are passionately in love.

As the hot summer wears on, Mitch and Blanche begin to date; she maintains a pose of genteel innocence which utterly charms him. She also describes her young husband's homosexuality and how her shocked reaction helped drive him to kill himself. Mitch's elderly mother is eager for him to find someone to be with after she dies and it seems these two lonely people might be able to comfort one another.

Meanwhile, however, Stanley has dug up the truth about Blanche's shady past in Laurel, which is a world away from the virginal act she has assumed for Mitch's benefit; her promiscuous behaviour was too much even for the Flamingo, the seedy low-rent hotel she called home, and she was evicted. Worse, she became involved with a 17-year-old pupil at her school; when the boy's father complained, she was instantly dismissed. Broke and homeless, Blanche was left with no one to turn to except Stella.

Stella is aghast when she finds that Stanley has told Mitch the truth about her sister, but he says he owed his old army buddy the truth. Mitch boycotts Blanche's birthday party on the afternoon of 15 September, while Stanley's 'gift' is a bus ticket back to Laurel. Another violent argument breaks out between the Kowalskis which ends abruptly when

Stella goes into labour. Stanley takes her to the hospital and Blanche is left alone in the apartment.

Later the same evening Mitch arrives to see Blanche, who has been drinking heavily. She tells him the truth about her past, hoping they can still be together, but he tells her she is not fit to marry and makes a clumsy attempt to rape her. Blanche fights him off and he leaves at once.

Now teetering on the edge of madness, Blanche believes she is about to leave New Orleans for a Caribbean cruise with her old beau Shep Huntleigh. Stanley returns home and tells her the baby will not be born until the morning. The tension between them finally explodes and although the frantic Blanche tries to defend herself with a broken bottle, Stanley disarms her easily and then rapes her.

Some weeks later Eunice is helping Stella with the baby while Stanley hosts another poker game. Stella tells Eunice that she cannot accept Blanche's story of the rape and go on living with Stanley; she has agreed to Blanche's being committed to a mental asylum. As the men play poker, Stella and Eunice collude with Blanche's fantasy that she is going to stay in the country. Blanche panics when a doctor and nurse arrive to take her away but eventually leaves calmly, escorted by the gentlemanly doctor. Stanley comforts the weeping Stella, but it seems he has good cause to believe that life will go on just as it did before Blanche came to New Orleans.

Scene summaries and commentaries

Scene I (pp. 3–15)

Context

New Orleans is divided into various districts, each with its own distinctive ambience; Elysian Fields is in the Vieux Carré or French Quarter, the most famous and atmospheric part of the city. During the late nineteenth and early twentieth centuries many immigrants settled here and the district developed a uniquely vibrant bohemian atmosphere, which makes it a major tourist attraction to this day.

It is early May in the shabby but vibrant working-class multicultural district of Elysian Fields in New Orleans. Two young men, Stanley Kowalski and Harold Mitchell, known as 'Mitch', arrive at the apartment Stanley shares with his wife, Stella. Stanley has brought home a package of butcher's meat which he tosses to Stella before he and Mitch leave for the bowling alley. Stella soon goes after them to watch. At this point a stranger arrives, carrying a suitcase; it is Stella's elder sister, Blanche DuBois. Eunice, Stella's neighbour and landlady, lets Blanche into the Kowalskis' apartment with her key while a Negro woman who had been chatting to Eunice offers to go and fetch Stella.

Once inside the apartment, it is clear Blanche thinks little of the cramped and untidy place and she is rather frosty with Eunice, who leaves her to herself. Blanche seems very highly strung and drinks a large whisky before carefully replacing the bottle and washing the glass. When Stella returns the sisters seem pleased to see each other, but Stella is worried by Blanche's hyperactive and excitable state; Blanche admits her bad nerves have forced her to take a leave of absence from her job as a schoolteacher in Laurel, Mississippi.

Blanche makes some extremely insensitive remarks about Stella's home, her looks and her working-class Polish-American husband. Stella strongly defends Stanley and is obviously madly in love with him. Blanche also tells Stella they have lost Belle Reve, the family's ancestral mansion in the country, describing the long-drawn-out decline and deaths of all their relatives and blaming Stella for leaving her to face things alone. Stella is reduced to tears and goes into the bathroom to wash her face.

Stanley arrives back from bowling and he and Blanche assess each other warily. He offers her a whisky, surprised by how little is left in the bottle; she refuses, telling him she rarely drinks. She is offended when he strips off his sweat-stained shirt in front of her. When Stanley asks about her husband, Blanche tells him that 'the boy' died, before declaring that she feels sick.

Task 1

Analyse how Williams arouses the reader's interest in this first scene.

A New Orleans streetcar like the one Blanche travelled on

Commentary: **The essence of drama is conflict, and here Williams introduces both the tragic protagonist of his drama and her antagonist. In this scene the audience may be confused by Blanche; on the one hand her hysterical narcissism, social snobbery and crass insensitivity are off-putting, but on the other it is clear that she is physically, emotionally and psychologically very frail. The contrast with her brother-in-law, the 'gaudy seed-bearer' (p. 14) Stanley, who hurls a package of meat at Stella like a primitive hunter returning with his kill, could hardly be more extreme. There is an obvious level of sexual innuendo underlying his words and actions which is confirmed by the raucous amusement of the Negro Woman and Eunice as well as Stella's excited response. Of Stella herself we learn relatively little, although it is clear both from the stage directions and her speech that she and Blanche are not of the same social class as the other characters who surround them. Although Blanche has come to stay with Stella and Stanley in Elysian Fields, she is a 'fish out of water': she is dressed as if for a party in the Garden District, where the wealthy aristocrats of the Old South built their grand mansions and looked down on the racially mixed inhabitants of the Vieux Carré.**

The audience hears two very different types of music in this scene which evoke both Blanche's new surroundings and her tragic past. Unlike the 'blue piano' music which is designed to suggest the atmosphere of New Orleans, the Varsouviana polka music is a non-naturalistic sound effect heard only in Blanche's imagination and by no other characters on stage. It symbolises

Context

Blanche relates the journey she has taken to reach Stella's home in 'Elysian Fields', riding a 'street-car named Desire' before transferring to another 'called Cemeteries'. In hindsight it seems clear that this journey is an allegorical representation of her tragic downfall, as in Greek mythology the Elysian Fields were a paradise for the dead.

Context

The 'blue piano' evokes the sound for which New Orleans has become world famous — so-called 'Dixieland' jazz and blues, a uniquely American blend of black African and European popular music which seems to embody the bohemian laid-back multicultural ambience of the city.

Pause for _Thought_ 𝕀𝕀

Because the French noun _rêve_, meaning 'dream', is masculine, the premodifying adjective meaning 'beautiful' should be _beau_ rather than _belle_. Does this 'mistake' suggest that there is, therefore, something slightly wrong with Blanche's 'beautiful dream' from the outset?

her husband's suicide, the tragic event which wrecked her life; hearing it sends her into an extreme state of panic and fear which only ends when she hears the terrible sound of a gunshot.

Already haunted by her young husband's suicide, Blanche describes the hideous dreams filled with the ghosts of her dead and dying relatives which sent her half-mad during her final years at Belle Reve. Because dreams cross the boundaries of waking and sleeping they encapsulate a liminal (threshold) state very suitable for exploring the shadowy borderlands of the imagination.

Scene II (pp. 15–24)

It is early evening on the day after Blanche's arrival in New Orleans. Blanche is taking a bath and Stella tells Stanley she is going to take Blanche out for the evening when he holds his poker night in the apartment. When Stella tells him that Belle Reve is lost Stanley suspects Blanche has swindled Stella (and thus him) out of her share of the estate and he insists on raking through Blanche's trunk looking for evidence. Stella tells him that while Blanche's faded finery may look expensive, actually it's all for show. Blanche emerges from the bathroom and flirts lightly with the sullen Stanley, but when she senses his suspicious mood she tries to protect Stella by asking her to fetch her a cool drink from the local drugstore. Blanche defends herself against Stanley's accusations and shows him the legal documents which relate to the loss of Belle Reve but he grabs some other papers from her trunk and begins to read them. Extremely distressed, Blanche seizes them back; they are her dead husband's love-letters. The legal documents prove that Belle Reve was lost when the DuBois family could no longer pay the mortgage and Blanche describes how her forebears drank, gambled and whored away everything until only the house itself and the family graveyard remained. Despite Stella's wish to keep the news from Blanche for a little longer, Stanley tells her that Stella is pregnant. Stella returns, the poker players arrive, and the two sisters head off for their evening out.

Pause for _Thought_ 𝕀𝕀

Think about different ways in which the confrontation between Blanche and Stanley might be directed, before watching the 1951 film version. Analyse which character you feel emerges as the more sympathetic in this interpretation and how you think the director, Elia Kazan, has tried to shape the audience's responses to each of them.

Commentary: **Blanche takes the first of her many long hot baths here, which — given that the cramped apartment has only one bathroom — seems very selfish behaviour from a long-term guest. The bathing symbolises Blanche's doomed attempt to erase her sordid past; compare her behaviour here with that of Shakespeare's Lady Macbeth, who compulsively washes imaginary bloodstains from her hands after Duncan's murder, to hide the 'evidence' of her crime.**

Stanley's resentful and suspicious attitude towards Blanche becomes increasingly clear in this scene and the audience may well find her more sympathetic than she at first appeared, given the tragic history of Belle Reve's decline and her current vulnerable position. Stanley senses that Blanche has invaded his territory and may prove a potential rival for Stella's affections; while he knows that Stella would never look at another man, given their passionate sexual connection, the arrival of his wife's last living blood relative threatens to raise the ghost of that aristocratic past from which Stanley has fought to isolate her. Beyond Stanley and Blanche's personal feelings for Stella lies a greater divide, that between the romanticised values and traditions of the Old South and the thrusting energetic pursuit of money and success in the postwar era, and both acknowledge the class divide between them. When Blanche says that she hurt her young husband the way that Stanley would like to hurt her, it seems to foreshadow his destruction of her social and sexual identity.

In terms of structure it is useful to note how Williams has artfully sectioned this scene into two parallel dialogues between Stanley and each of the sisters; we see him baffled and angered by the superior knowledge and understanding of first Stella and then Blanche.

> ## Task **2**
>
> Compare and contrast the way in which Blanche describes the loss of Belle Reve to Stanley in this scene with her speech about the same event to Stella in Scene I.

> ## Pause for **Thought** ❙❙
>
> What do you think might be the possible effects upon an audience of this juxtapositioning of dialogues?

Scene III 'The Poker Night' (pp. 24–34)

Blanche and Stella return after their girls' night out to find the poker night in full swing. When his best friend Mitch leaves the game to talk to Blanche, Stanley throws a drunken tantrum and hurls a radio out of the

Photostage

The poker night, as performed in the 2009 London production of the play

Taking it Further

Tennessee Williams called an earlier draft of the play 'The Poker Night', which underlines the importance of this scene. The stage directions refer to an 1888 painting by the Dutch Expressionist artist Vincent Van Gogh called *The Night Café*. You can view this painting at www.turgingsomedrama. com/streetcar/ streetcarbackground.htm

Taking it Further

Watch this scene in two of the film versions listed in the 'Taking it further' section (pp. 92–94 of this book). Which do you find the most powerful, and why?

Pause for *Thought*

During Scene III the music begins to mirror the violent dramatic action on stage; dissonant *'brass and piano sounds'* are heard and a *'low-tone clarinet moans'* (p. 33). What do you think the music can add to the audience's understanding of the stormy emotions at work here?

window. Stella is furious at his coarse and aggressive behaviour and he is violent towards her. The sisters escape upstairs to Eunice's, but Stella returns to Stanley when he pleads for her and they go to bed. Mitch finds a distressed Blanche outside and tries to comfort her.

Commentary: **This is one of only two scenes in the play in which nearly all the characters appear — the other is Scene XI — and the only one which has its own title, 'The Poker Night'. Stanley is the leader of the pack and lord of all he surveys; his drunken bullying violence creates a sense of increasing danger and menace as he controls the scene. The poker game is a vivid and ominous metaphor for the game of life itself, as it involves bluffing, playing the hand you've been dealt, taking your chances when they come and riding any streak of luck that happens to come your way.**

When Stella calls Stanley an 'animal thing' (p. 31) and runs from his drunken and bestial rage in fear, his primal roar of 'STELL-LAHHHHHH!' into the night has her returning to her savage mate as *'they come together with low, animal moans'* (p. 33). Stella's passionate loyalty to her husband bodes ill for Blanche. The passionate relationship between Stanley and Stella is paralleled by Mitch's attraction to Blanche's mysterious aura of gentility and there is some comedy here amid the violence as the ladylike French-speaking belle dances with the awkward, shambling average Joe. They make an odd couple, and even though both have loved and lost, it seems a bad omen that, whereas Mitch is simple, honest and serious, Blanche is complex, deceitful and flighty.

Scene IV (pp. 34–41)

Despite Blanche's passionate attempts to persuade Stella to leave Stanley after the poker night debacle, Stella insists that she loves him. Blanche suggests that she and Stella contact a millionaire named Shep Huntleigh who can help them escape. Unknown to the sisters, Stanley has returned to the apartment and has overheard Blanche's harsh and hostile comments about him.

Commentary: **While Stella does not try to justify Stanley's aggressive behaviour, it is clear to Blanche (and to the audience) that she is sexually excited by his macho persona; she recalls their wedding night, when he smashed all the light-bulbs using her shoe, with delight, although Blanche is horrified by his brutality. It seems ironic that the aristocratic DuBois sisters —**

Southern belles born and bred — have both ridden the literal and metaphorical streetcar which 'bangs through the Quarter, up one old narrow street and down another'; while Blanche now bitterly regrets this, however, Stella is still joyfully revelling in the journey. Blanche's painful admission, 'It [the streetcar] brought me here' (p. 40), refers not only to her scandalous past in Laurel, but also reaches further back in time: Blanche and Stella are the last of a family infamous for their 'epic fornications' (p. 22). Despite the fact that the audience has just witnessed Stanley at his very worst, Blanche's cynical plan to inveigle Shep Huntleigh into financing their getaway makes it less easy to believe that she wants to leave New Orleans solely for Stella's sake. Williams creates a level of intense dramatic irony in this scene: while the audience is aware of Stanley's sinister eavesdropping, the two women remain totally unaware of his presence. It is clear that Blanche's hysterical outburst will provoke him to strike back at his enemy, knowing that while he may have triumphed in this particular battle, he still has to win the war.

❮ Top ten *quotation*

*Pause for **Thought***

Read the final stage directions in this scene (p. 41). How and why does this tableau render dialogue unnecessary here?

Scene V (pp. 42–49)

In the apartment upstairs Eunice and Steve are fighting about Steve's alleged infidelity. Blanche is terrified when Stanley hints that he knows the truth about her past. Eunice and Steve make up and Stanley goes out for a drink at the Four Deuces. Blanche tells Stella how much she dreads growing old alone and that she is thinking about a safe future with Mitch. After Stella follows Stanley, Steve and Eunice to the bar, Blanche kisses a young man who arrives to collect a newspaper subscription before Mitch (whom she calls her '*Rosenkavalier*') arrives to take her out on a date.

Commentary: **This is a scene of inexorably building tension. When Stanley mentions the travelling salesman Shaw who knew Blanche from the Flamingo Hotel she knows the act she has been putting on for Mitch's benefit is in danger of unravelling, while her sexual attraction to the unknown young man is so inappropriate that in this context even the coarse and brutal relationship of Steve and Eunice looks 'normal'. In flirting with the young man Blanche reveals how much of her essential nature she is struggling to repress in order to play the part of Mitch's 'prim and proper' prospective fiancée. Her behaviour clearly foreshadows the revelation of the real reason she was run out of Laurel, although here she just manages to control herself: 'Run along now!...I've got to be good and keep my hands off children'**

Context

The heroine of Richard Strauss's 1911 opera *Der Rosenkavalier* ('The Knight of the Rose') is the beautiful and aristocratic Marschallin, who eventually surrenders her young lover to another woman. This reference makes it clear that having just bid farewell to the Young Man, Blanche sees herself as a second gallant Marschallin who will live to fight another day.

(p. 49). Blanche, an 'epic fornicator' like all the rest of her family, hopes that marrying Mitch will help keep the lid on her wayward sexual desires.

Scene VI (pp. 50–57)

Blanche and Mitch's date is not a great success; her nerves are in tatters at the thought of Stanley revealing the truth about her. At the end of the evening, however, they open up to each other and Blanche tells him about her young husband. Tortured by his homosexuality, Allan shot himself in the mouth after she found him with another man and revealed her disgust at his behaviour. Mitch comforts Blanche and tells her that they should be together: 'Could it be — you and me, Blanche?'

Top ten *quotation* ❯

Commentary: **Blanche's encounter with the Young Man in the previous scene is juxtaposed with the very different way she orchestrates her relationship with Mitch here. She scripts a scene in which she can play the role of the tragic courtesan Marguerite to Mitch's innocent Armand, showing yet again her tendency to wilful self-dramatisation. The richness and complexity of Williams's dramaturgy is shown in his merging of aural and verbal symbolism; as the Varsouviana polka music plays in the background to externalise the memory of Allan's death, Blanche tells Mitch how falling in love had illuminated her world with a 'blinding light' which was brutally extinguished when he killed himself.**

While Blanche is technically Mitch's social and intellectual superior, it shows how far she has fallen that she now needs him far more than he needs her. What Blanche chooses to reveal and conceal here is crucial. Telling Mitch the shocking truth about Allan's suicide in fact brings them closer, because Mitch has also loved and lost; indeed his sympathetic response may suggest that if Blanche had been equally frank about the aspects of her past she continues to withhold from him, he might just have forgiven these too. However, Blanche's failure to let in the light here foreshadows the end of their tentative relationship, because what she has decided must remain hidden Stanley is sure to disclose.

Task 3

Write an alternative ending for Scene VI in which Blanche begins, tentatively, to tell Mitch the truth about her life in Laurel. You should aim to build upon Williams's presentation of both Blanche and Mitch and capture aspects of his chosen form, structure and language. You might wish to write a brief commentary to accompany your work, explaining how and where you have tried to reflect the source text.

Scene VII (pp. 58–63)

It is a *'late afternoon in mid-September'* and Stella is preparing a birthday meal for Blanche. Stanley arrives home and while Blanche sings happily to herself in the bathroom, he reveals what he has discovered about her past. After the loss of Belle Reve, Blanche had moved into a low-rent hotel called the Flamingo, from which she was eventually evicted because of her promiscuous behaviour; she had been fired from her teaching post because an angry parent told the principal that Blanche was having an affair with his 17-year-old son. To Stella's horror, Stanley has told Mitch everything.

Commentary: **After the apparently hopeful ending of the previous scene, this one seems to begin positively as Stella prepares a birthday supper and Blanche warbles away in the bathroom. Yet the mood completely changes as Stanley arrives home in triumph with proof of Blanche's sexual misbehaviour; once more Williams creates intense dramatic contrast. Blanche's failure to be honest with Mitch at the end of the previous scene was undoubtedly cowardly and deceitful, yet the audience is surely aware that Stanley, when allocating the blame for her downfall, is motivated by more than simply an honest desire to protect Mitch. The fact that Stanley metaphorically stabs Blanche in the back by telling Stella the truth without giving her a chance to defend herself recalls Scene IV, when he deliberately concealed himself to eavesdrop on the sisters; on both occasions he reveals the kind of animal cunning that makes him such a dangerous enemy.**

Williams creates a brilliantly uneasy mismatch here as moments of black comedy blur into a far more disturbing picture. Yet again — and with some justification — Stanley is driven crazy by Blanche's 'Washing out some things' and 'Soaking in a hot tub' (p. 58) in his bathroom; when she asks him to wait a little longer — 'Possess your soul in patience!' — he replies 'It's not my soul I'm worried about' (p. 61), implying he needs to use the toilet. Yet lurking below this crude humour is a sinister metaphorical wish to soil the place in which Blanche seeks to purify herself. Once again music serves to heighten tension and create dramatic irony, by juxtaposing Blanche's singing with Stanley's remorseless demolition of her fantasy future with Mitch. Note that Williams's stage directions show that Blanche's singing and Stanley's revelation of the truth about her take place 'contrapuntally'; the term contrapuntal is used here to convey the unbridgeable gulf between the two enemies and the melodramatic — almost operatic — heightened tension of the scene. Stella's increasingly panic-stricken clichés — 'Lower your voice!'; 'What — contemptible — lies!'; 'It's pure invention!'; 'I

contrapuntal
a description of polyphonic music in which the various parts are very clearly differentiated; in marked contrast to the original melody

Taking it Further ►

The song 'Paper Moon' symbolises Blanche's relationship with Mitch. As she sings 'It's a Barnum and Bailey world/Just as phony as it can be/ But it wouldn't be make-believe/If you believed in me' it seems clear her future happiness depends on Mitch's continuing to believe that the act she's been putting on for his benefit is real. You can listen to Nat King Cole perform the song at **www.youtube.com/ watch?v=OKxWpZzf09M**.

Pause for Thought ⏸

Think about alternative ways of performing this scene which might suggest different motivations for Stanley's actions and thus other ways of interpreting his character. Work with a group of students if possible.

don't want to hear any more!' (pp. 59–60) — show that she is in deep denial. Ominously, Stanley reveals to Stella that the inhabitants of Laurel believed Blanche to be mad as well as bad; his contact Shaw heard she was regarded 'as not just different but downright loco — nuts' (p. 60). Later, when he tells Stella that he has bought Blanche a ticket back to Laurel for the following Tuesday he declares, 'Her future is mapped out for her' (p. 63). Thanks to him, this is wholly true.

Scene VIII (pp. 64–69)

'Three-quarters of an hour later' Blanche, Stella and Stanley are seated around the birthday table, but Mitch's chair is empty. It is clear that he has rejected Blanche following Stanley's revelation of the truth about her past. The tension builds until Stanley gives Blanche her birthday present — the ticket back to Laurel. Stella is appalled by Stanley's brutal malice and they argue fiercely about Blanche once more. The situation brings on Stella's labour and immediately Stanley takes her to hospital, leaving Blanche alone in the apartment.

Commentary: **By now the conflict is ratcheting up towards the play's dramatic climax as Stanley determines to kick Blanche out of the apartment. For the first time she defends herself when he insults her. Stella, angrier than we have ever seen her before, tells Stanley that Blanche was innocent and trusting before 'people like you abused her' (p. 68), which surely implies that she expects Stanley to make her sister suffer too. Perhaps Stanley's animal magnetism has already changed Stella — or just liberated something similar which was already buried deep inside her. Williams uses the Kowalskis' dialogue to stress the growing gulf between them at this point; as Stella's speech becomes more formal and educated, Stanley's becomes more and more colloquial and fragmentary. Although the play predates it by about 25 years, in sociolinguistic terms the Kowalskis' dialogue in this scene can be seen as a fictional representation of Howard Giles' Communication Accommodation Theory (CAT). This theory examines how and why people alter their speech to stress or minimise their social differences. Giles argues that when speakers feel positive and cooperative their speech styles tend to converge to create rapport, whereas when they are at odds with each other they tend to diverge as they move to emphasise the social distance between them.**

Stella's disgusted attack on Stanley's table manners sends him into a fury because it so clearly demonstrates the radical difference between the sisters' upbringing and his own; using an image drawn from the game of poker he yells, 'What do you two think you are? A pair of queens?' (p. 65).

Stanley reminds Stella how he changed her from a genteel Southern belle initially repulsed by his crude passion into a willing sexual partner:

> When we first met, me and you, you thought I was common. How right you was, baby. I was common as dirt. You showed me the snapshot of the place with the columns. I pulled you down off them columns and how you loved it, having them coloured lights going! And wasn't we happy together, wasn't it all okay till she showed here? (p. 68)

❮ Top ten **quotation**

These words indicate that it is a jealous fear of Blanche which makes him so determined to destroy her.

Stella's anger at Stanley's cruelty represents a potential rebellion which is cut short when she goes into labour. The timing of this event is a massive stroke of luck for him, as the baby symbolises their unbreakable connection and is Stella's main reason for finally siding with him against her sister. Over and above this, Stella's labour ensures that Blanche will be left alone and unprotected in the apartment. Note that the Varsouviana polka is used differently at the end of this scene; *'rising with sinister rapidity'* (p. 69), it is no longer linked solely with the death of Allan Grey, but presages another defining crisis in Blanche's life. Ominously, at the beginning of the next scene, the Varsouviana becomes 'rapid' and 'feverish'.

Scene IX (pp. 69–75)

'A while later that evening' Mitch arrives and challenges Blanche about what Stanley has told him. Blanche says that while the stories are true, she was seeking love and comfort after the death of her husband and wanted to escape the harsh world in which she found herself. Mitch rejects her as unfit to be his wife and live in the same house as his dying mother. He tries to force her to have sex but when she shouts 'Fire! Fire! Fire!' (p. 75) out of the window he leaves at once.

Commentary: **When Mitch turns on the light it is an aggressive act designed to unveil the 'real' Blanche hidden behind the**

*Pause for **Thought***

Do you think it is significant, given Stanley's ethnicity, that *Varsouviana* means 'from Warsaw' (the capital of Poland) and that this polka was originally a Polish peasant dance? If so, what are your reasons? Think about why Williams chose this simple, sentimental tune to express such heightened and complex emotions. You can listen to it being played at **www.youtube.com**; search for 'Varsouviana County Fair'.

old-fashioned Southern belle persona she has relied upon to charm him. On their previous date she lit a candle to make believe they were in Paris, the city of romance; now Mitch turns on a much harsher light which destroys her false veneer of respectability and prefigures his attempt to rape her.

The appearance of the Mexican flower seller in this scene terrifies Blanche, who presumably interprets her cry of *'Flores para los muertos'* ('flowers for the dead') as an eerie premonition of her own fate.

This scene, which was apparently Williams's own favourite, brilliantly juxtaposes black comedy and lyrical tragedy. Blanche's vivid dialogue encompasses a scornful description of herself living at a hotel called the 'Tarantula Arms' like 'a big spider! That's where I brought my victims!' (p. 73) as well as a poignantly lyrical description of Mitch as 'a cleft in the rock of the world that I could hide in!' (p. 73). Blanche had pinned all her hopes on marrying Mitch because she had hoped it would prevent her hitching another ride on the fatal 'street-car named Desire', but his rejection signals the death of all her hopes for a peaceful and secure future. Blanche's lies are an escapist strategy designed to block out a reality she finds too harsh to bear, but with no one left to lie to, her only remaining audience is herself.

*Pause for **Thought***

Do you find the potent visual symbolism of the flower seller too melodramatic here, or do you think Williams's use of this device can be justified in terms of its powerful effect?

Top ten *quotation*〉

*Pause for **Thought***

As Blanche's make-believe world crumbles, so does Williams's set. Three New Orleans characters are visible to both Blanche and the audience: a prostitute, an alcoholic and a thief. How far can these characters be seen as representations of Blanche herself and what is your response to Williams's use of visual symbolism here?

Scene X (pp. 75–81)

Stanley returns from the hospital to find Blanche dressed for a society ball. Drunk and delusional, she informs him she will soon be leaving for a Caribbean cruise with her former beau, the Texas oil millionaire Shep Huntleigh. The sexual tension which has been building between them for months begins to spiral out of control as Stanley puts on the silk pyjamas he wore on his wedding night. As she tries to get past him Stanley blocks her way; the terrified Blanche smashes a bottle and threatens to slash his face with it. Stanley grabs her and carries her to the bed to rape her, declaring 'We've had this date with each other from the beginning!' (p. 81).

Commentary: **Drunk, confused and wearing a *'soiled and crumpled'* party dress she would normally have been ashamed to be seen in (p. 75), Blanche makes a horribly sad Cinderella figure here, shuffling about in her 'scuffed silver slippers' talking to the only audience she has left — herself. At first it seems Stanley has returned from the hospital in a reasonably friendly mood, but, as so often, they misunderstand each other,** and the atmosphere quickly turns poisonous. Blanche tries to telephone for help, but the external world is once again presented as a dangerous jungle which can offer no support.

There is a tension between the immediate build-up to Stanley's assault on Blanche, which seems haphazard and unplanned, and its dramatic function as the inevitable climax of their deadly power struggle. Stanley's comment that they have 'had this date from the beginning' ties in with Williams's decision to have the rape take place off stage; there is no room for doubt as to whether this act has actually taken place, given that it has been so clearly foreshadowed by his invasion of Blanche's private possessions — including her love-letters from Allan — at the beginning of the play. Moreover, since sexual domination has always been Stanley's modus operandi when it comes to dealing with Stella, the utterly taboo act of raping her sister has a hideous internal logic. The sexual desire he has discovered and stoked within Stella is twisted into a nightmarish kind of 'incest by proxy' as he costumes himself once again in the silk pyjamas he bought for his wedding-night.

❮ Top ten *quotation*

There is an uncomfortable grain of truth in Stanley's declaration that he and Blanche had had their 'date' from the beginning; the seething tension between them might have been expressed most often in social, economic and cultural terms, but there was always something deeply sexual about his prurient interest in her promiscuous past and her coyly flirtatious response to his macho posturing. Before attacking her physically, Stanley first rapes her emotionally and psychologically by demolishing her pathetic Shep Huntleigh fantasy, as if to underline the fact that sex with him is her only option. In this context, Stanley's brutality seems so extreme and all-encompassing that the rape can be seen to represent the annihilation of the Old South by the thrusting postwar world.

A much less cynical and nihilistic take on the inevitable destruction of Blanche's world is encapsulated in the florid epigraph to the 1939 film of Margaret Mitchell's romantic saga *Gone With The Wind* (1936). As the credits roll, iconic images evoking the spirit of the Old South provide the backdrop, including peaceful fields being farmed by contented slaves, the majestic Mississippi river and a gaudy scarlet sunset. You can watch the opening credits of the film online at: www.youtube. com/watch?v=48o5sq2PUGw

Immediately after the title credits roll, the film begins with this nostalgic elegy:

> There was a land of Cavaliers and Cotton Fields called the Old South. Here in this pretty world, Gallantry took its last bow. Here was the last ever to be seen of Knights and their Ladies Fair, of Master and of Slave. Look for it only in books, for it is no more than a dream remembered; a Civilization gone with the wind...

Scene XI (pp. 81–90)

'*Some weeks later*' Stella and Eunice are packing Blanche's trunk while she finishes bathing and the men play poker. They are awaiting the arrival of a doctor and nurse to take Blanche to an insane asylum, but Blanche, who has clearly crossed the border into outright madness by now, thinks she is going to the country to visit Shep Huntleigh. Stella tells Eunice she cannot allow herself to believe Blanche's assertion that Stanley raped her, and Eunice reassures her that she has no other choice: 'Life has got to go on' (p. 83). When the doctor and nurse arrive, Blanche panics. Stanley and his friends subdue Blanche as Eunice holds Stella back; Mitch begins to cry and accuses Stanley of having reduced Blanche to this state, while the other men also mutter uncomfortably. Finally, the gentlemanly doctor earns Blanche's trust ('I have always depended on the kindness of strangers', p. 89) and she leaves quietly. Stella sobs bitterly, hugging the baby as Stanley tries to comfort her. The play ends as Steve announces, 'This game is seven-card stud' (p. 90). Life in Elysian Fields, it seems, will go on as if Blanche DuBois had never been there at all.

Commentary: **After the previous climactic rape scene, Scene XI is a kind of coda. In many ways this sombre and downbeat scene — in which all the main characters appear for only the second time — functions as a grotesque inversion of the poker night, in which the electrifying excitement of the drunken, violent Stanley being wrangled into the shower by his buddies is horrifyingly re-enacted as the pitiful, terrified Blanche is wrestled to the floor before being taken off to the asylum.**

Blanche does not wish to pass Stanley and his poker buddies on her way through the apartment as they are by now irrelevant to her; the last of her trademark long hot baths suggests she now wishes ritually to wash away the 'stain' of her rape in order to be 'pure' for her imaginary beau, Shep Huntleigh. Blanche's desire

Context

For further information on the American South and on Tennessee Williams as a Southern writer, see the *Themes* and *Contexts* sections of this guide.

Top ten **quotation** ❭

Top ten **quotation** ❭

Top ten **quotation** ❭

coda a dramatic postscript or afterthought

to appear innocent and virginal is symbolised by her choice of costume for her departure; although Eunice compliments the 'pretty blue jacket', which Stella thinks is 'lilac coloured', Blanche declares: 'You're both mistaken. It's Della Robbia blue. The blue of the robe in the old Madonna pictures' (p. 84).

Given that Stanley mocked Blanche as 'the Queen of the Nile' (p. 79) earlier in the play, it is interesting that Shakespeare's indelible image of Cleopatra preparing for death, attended by her two faithful handmaidens, is evoked here. Unlike Charmian and Iras, however, who both choose to die along with their mistress, the loyalty of Stella and Eunice is fatally compromised. While it seems that Blanche has finally given up trying to reinvent reality and has blocked it out once and for all, she is not the only woman in an extreme state of denial here. Stella might as well sing her baby to sleep with 'Paper Moon', as she has willingly decided to live in a fantasy world; denying Blanche's story and believing in her 'madness' allows Stella to avoid the truth about her husband. While their gentle kindness towards Blanche suggests that at some deep level they both know the truth, Stella and Eunice also know that that truth must remain unspoken so life can go on. Steve's comment 'This game is seven-card stud' (p. 90) highlights the idea that while men seem to hold all the cards, women are forced to collude with them and pretend to believe their hollow bluffing.

Like Blanche, who is wearing 'Della Robbia blue', Stella's baby son is wrapped in a pale blue blanket which makes the triptych of mother, father and child at the end of the play a warped visual image of the Holy Family. Yet in this Darwinist 'survival of the fittest' society in which Blanche must be sacrificed to ensure Stanley's future, Williams questions whether everything is really as secure as it may seem. While Stella and Eunice know deep down that the baby represents the future and that therefore his need for security must take precedence, should we not fear, given that Stanley's behaviour is often extremely childlike, that one day Stanley will become just as jealous of his son's ties to Stella as he was of Blanche's?

❮ Top ten *quotation*

▌ *Pause for **Thought*** ⏸

In Charlotte Brontë's *Jane Eyre*, written 100 years before *A Streetcar Named Desire*, another wife (Jane) asserts the madness of her husband's sexual partner (i.e. his dead wife) to justify his oppressive actions towards her 'rival' and legitimise her own continuing relationship with the father of her child. You might compare these two texts and look at the extent to which their treatment of this similar theme reflects their radically different contemporary cultural milieux.

Themes

Pause for **Thought** ❙❙

According to Christopher Innes, *Streetcar* contains all of Williams's 'major themes: the ambiguous nature of sexuality, the betrayal of faith, the corruption of modern America, the over-arching battle of artistic sensitivity against physical materialism' (Innes in S. McEvoy, *Tragedy: A Student Handbook*, 2009).

Pause for **Thought** ❙❙

In both F. Scott Fitzgerald's *The Great Gatsby* (1925) and John Steinbeck's *Of Mice and Men* (1936) the tragic central characters' dreams are ended with a violent gunshot. Look at these two novels and think about how far you agree that they — and *Streetcar* — present dreams as transient and illusory, but rare and valuable nonetheless.

The Italian author Primo Levi declared in his book *Other People's Trades* (1989) that 'all authors have had the opportunity of being astonished by the beautiful and awful things that the critics have found in their works and that they did not know they had put there'. Often, we have no means of knowing an author's intentions; what is important is the impact of the text on a reader or, in the case of a play, an audience. Even if an author has written explicitly about what he or she sees as the key thematic content of a work, that does not preclude other themes from coming to the attention of particular readers. Moreover, Williams's work cannot be divorced from the circumstances of his life, values, assumptions, gender, race and class, and just as he was a product of his age, so you are a product of yours. How you respond to *A Streetcar Named Desire* will depend on your own experiences, ideas and values and it is well worth thinking about how readers and audiences decide what the major themes of any literary text are.

Reality and illusion

Williams's famously poetic stage directions, in which Blanche is likened to a fluttering white moth who must avoid the light, suggest that she craves 'magic' because the truth about postwar America is too harsh to bear. Her antagonist Stanley, on the other hand, is imbued with an earthy — even brutal — sense of realism which makes him loathe her 'Barnum and Bailey world' and do all he can to trash it. Thus the theme of fantasy and reality plays out on stage as another aspect of the desperate struggle between the play's protagonist and antagonist. Which character you decide to side with is up to you. When Stanley rapes Blanche he uses the disturbingly incongruous word 'date' to describe what he has planned for her, as if they are lovers who have passed a pleasant evening in each other's company; thus he ensures that her Shep Huntleigh illusion is utterly destroyed. The question of how far illusions are helpful or necessary remains; ironically, as Felicia Hardison Londré notes, it is only when Blanche actually tells Mitch the truth for once — about the death of Allan Grey — that she finally gains 'what she has not been able to achieve in two months or so of artful deceit: a proposal of marriage' (Londré in M. Roudané, *The Cambridge Companion to Tennessee Williams*, 1997).

Death and desire

Streetcar was one of the first postwar dramas to present a range of characters for whom sex was of huge importance as a factor influencing their lives and relationships. One of the text's defining images — that of the streetcar — explicitly links sex and death, making it possible to see the play within the context of the **Liebestod** tradition.

At first glance it might seem a struggle to position *Streetcar* within this literary framework (after all, nobody dies at the end) but in fact the *Liebestod* theme may be seen to enhance (or parody) the romantic and tragic grandeur of Blanche's downfall, depending on your point of view.

Very early in the play the English teacher Blanche makes the first of her evocative and suggestive literary references when she likens the chain of events which culminated in the loss of Belle Reve to something 'Only Poe! Only Mr. Edgar Allan Poe!' could conceive (p. 8), as her DuBois forebears went to rack and ruin through indulging in their 'epic fornications' (p. 22). The specific situation to which she refers here — the fall of a once great family and their home — calls to mind Poe's Gothic horror story *The Fall of the House of Usher* (1839), with Blanche as the persecuted Madeline who is entombed, while still alive, by her twin brother. Blanche's awareness of her own fate is signalled by her horrified reaction to the Mexican Woman with her flowers for the dead, and while Stanley is her brother-in-law and not her brother, his rape does indeed consign her to a kind of death-in-life which seems to resemble Madeline's as she is 'entombed' within the walls of a lunatic asylum.

Like her husband Allan, whose homosexuality led directly to his death, Blanche is a figure for whom sex and death are fatally entwined. Following Allan's suicide, Blanche is left with a morbid fear of ageing, and in some ways her attraction to very young men suggests that in seducing them she hopes to recapture something of her own lost youth and innocence. Yet the love (or sex, or desire) with which Blanche tries to fight off death is also the direct cause of her tragic fall, the sickness as well as the cure.

On several further occasions throughout the play, literary references are used to evoke images of famous women, real and fictional, who have suffered and died for love. Introducing herself to Mitch during Stanley's poker night, Blanche tells him that she's an English teacher struggling to 'instil a bunch of bobby-soxers and drug-store Romeos with reverence for Hawthorne and Whitman and Poe!' (p. 31). The reference to 'Romeos'

Liebestod

(from the German meaning 'love death') an erotic union achieved by lovers only through or after death

Context

Two of the most famous texts from within the English literary tradition to deal with the *Liebestod* theme are Shakespeare's *Romeo and Juliet* (*c.* 1595) and Emily Brontë's *Wuthering Heights* (1847), while in Stephenie Meyer's popular teenage *Twilight* series, the heroine, Bella Swan, can only achieve a permanent relationship with Edward Cullen after she too has become a vampire.

Context

Blanche likens her experiences at Belle Reve to the Gothic horror stories of Edgar Allan Poe (1809–49). Poe, who died in poverty at the age of 40, was a master of the short story. *The Fall of the House of Usher* is a characteristic work that you might enjoy reading; another is *The Masque of the Red Death*.

The American novelist Nathaniel Hawthorne (1804–64) often explored the darker side of human existence in his morally and psychologically intricate works, the most famous of which is *The Scarlet Letter.*

Top ten **quotation** ❯

is doubly ironic, in view of her fatal attraction to underage boys, while the mention of Nathaniel Hawthorne evokes the image of Hester Prynne, the heroine of his most famous novel *The Scarlet Letter* (1850), who is shunned and scorned by her narrow-minded Puritan community for adultery and fornication.

Later Blanche assumes the role of the doomed courtesan Marguerite, heroine of Dumas' tragic romance *La Dame aux Camélias,* casting the hapless Mitch as her much younger lover, Armand, before referring to his physical strength by calling him 'Samson', a reference to the Old Testament strongman betrayed by the fatal temptress Delilah. Finally, and perhaps most ominously, however, it is Stanley who provides the last literary figure with whom we are invited to compare *Streetcar*'s doomed heroine. He viciously parodies Blanche's 'hoity-toity' affectations by likening her to Cleopatra: '...lo and behold the place has turned into Egypt and you are the Queen of the Nile!' (p. 79).

Marginality and madness: the outcast

According to Alycia Smith-Howard and Greta Heintzelman, Williams 'is celebrated as "a poet of the human heart" and as the "Laureate of the Outcast"' (Smith-Howard and Heintzelman, *Critical Companion to Tennessee Williams,* 2005). In 1939 the playwright told his literary agent Audrey Wood, 'I have only one major theme for my work, which is the destructive power of society on the sensitive non-conformist individual' and in *Streetcar* Blanche is indeed cast out of society because she refuses to conform to conventional moral values. Forced to confess her sins, she is then viciously punished.

Top ten **quotation** ❯

The ancient Greek word for tragedy means 'goat-song' and Blanche is surely the scapegoat here, cast out of society in order to bear the sins of others. While Stanley, previously dismissed as an uncouth 'Polack', is socially on the up, Blanche is gradually stripped of her psychological, sexual, financial and cultural identity. At the end of the play, Blanche is forced to retreat into madness in order to shield her fragile sense of self from Stanley's brutal truth.

Characters

One of the most common errors made by students is to write about characters in literature as if they were real people as opposed to fictional constructs created to fulfil a range of purposes in different texts. When it comes to a play, the 'language' belonging to each character is a blueprint for their interpretation by different actors, and one important aspect of analysis is to consider the range of potential performances of a text.

Characters in a play are defined through language and action. What they do, what they say, how they say it, and what other characters say about them determine the response of a reader. On stage these techniques of characterisation are enhanced by costume, gesture, facial expression, proxemics (the distance between actors which indicates the relationship between the characters) and other performance features.

As well as the brief sketches below, there is more information about the main characters in several other sections of this book, particularly the *Scene summaries and commentaries*, *Themes* and *Contexts*.

*Pause for **Thought*** ⏸

Look at the painting *Poker Night (from A Streetcar Named Desire)* (1948) by Thomas Hart Benton (1889–1975): go to **http://whitney.org** and click on Collection — B — Thomas Hart Benton. Jessica Tandy, who created the role of Blanche, felt that this overtly sexualised image was a misrepresentation. Do you agree?

Blanche DuBois

For many Williams fans, Blanche DuBois is his quintessential heroine, psychologically damaged, emotionally fragile, socially liminal and culturally dispossessed. When Eunice first sees her dressed in those utterly incongruous floating white clothes she asks: 'What's the matter, honey? Are you lost?' (p. 5). Indeed she is; in fact Blanche is the archetypal lost soul, but Williams makes her an insensitive, prickly and often irritating character rather than one the audience necessarily identifies with and pities from the outset. Blanche is an ageing Southern belle on the wrong side of 30, whose tragic and stormy life has led her to avoid reality in favour of what she dreamily

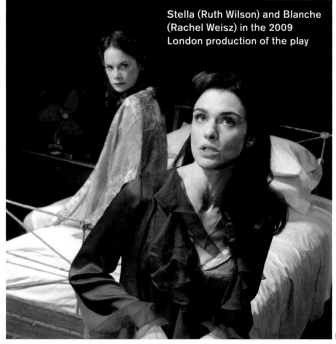

Stella (Ruth Wilson) and Blanche (Rachel Weisz) in the 2009 London production of the play

Photostage

Taking it Further ▶

Williams's presentation of sexual tension and class conflict as inextricably linked in the downfall of an iconic female protagonist echoes both Henrik Ibsen's *Hedda Gabler* (1890) and August Strindberg's *Miss Julie* (1888). Look at one or both of these plays. What similarities and differences in plot and character can you trace?

Top ten **quotation** ▶

Pause for **Thought** ⏸

Depending on how Stella is played, her character could come across as more or less sympathetic. How would you choose to present her if you were directing the play, and what elements of Williams's characterisation and dialogue would sway your decision?

refers to as 'magic'. As the play progresses, Blanche's instability grows as Stanley strips away her fantasy life and wrecks her relationship with Mitch. Haunted by all she has lost — her first love, her home, her culture, her dignity and her place in the world — her life is already a sexual, emotional and economic disaster zone when she arrives in Elysian Fields. Underneath her unpleasantly snobbish arrogance lies a vulnerable and damaged psyche. Loneliness and a lack of self-esteem has led her to come close to prostitution and she sees marrying Mitch as her only way out. However, Stanley's merciless persecution of her culminates in a brutal rape which triggers her complete mental breakdown.

Stanley Kowalski

Proud to be a second-generation Polish American, at the beginning of the play Stanley Kowalski appears to be a loyal friend, a passionate husband and a genial host. A decorated soldier who fought in the Second World War, Stanley is down-to-earth, forceful and practical; Blanche's genteel fictions and fantasies drive him crazy. At first he may well have the audience's sympathy when Blanche ignorantly refers to him as a 'Polack', and it is not hard to see that his hatred of her stems from the genteel Southern past she represents as well as her infuriating airs and graces. As time goes on, however, Stanley's behaviour towards Blanche becomes increasingly hostile and vicious to the point where it is clearly unjustified by any of her actions. By the time the play ends the audience has witnessed Stanley bullying his friends, abusing his pregnant wife and raping his fragile sister-in-law. The final tableau of Stanley soothing the sobbing Stella may be seen to pose uncomfortable questions about the criteria by which Blanche has been socially excluded.

Stella Kowalski

Stella's name embodies the tension between her former life at Belle Reve and her new life in Elysian Fields; Blanche's 'Stella for star' has become Stanley's 'STELLLAHHHH!' Unlike her sister, Stella got away from Belle Reve during the war and made her way to New Orleans where she met Stanley; only during a time of such immense social, cultural and historical upheaval would the aristocratic Stella DuBois have met the working-class Stanley Kowalski. Like her sister, Stella is a sexually passionate woman and although she pities Blanche and wants to protect her, she refuses to allow herself to believe her accusation of rape. Stella's decision to go for fantasy over reality in the end seems to indicate that she is a DuBois born and bred after all.

Harold 'Mitch' Mitchell

Though on the surface Mitch seems lumbering, gauche and ungainly, he is a sensitive and kindly soul at heart. Teased as a 'mama's boy', Mitch wants to marry so that his mother can die in peace, knowing that he won't be left alone after her death. Mitch and Blanche, having both loved and lost, believe they can comfort one another. When Stanley tells him the truth about Blanche's past, however, Mitch feels Blanche has made a fool of him with her virginal Southern belle act and tries to force her to sleep with him; he weeps when she is taken away to the asylum. While some readers and audiences may see Mitch as a clownish character, others may view him as a tragic figure in his own right.

Eunice Hubbel

Stella's friend, neighbour and landlady, Eunice may foreshadow the life Stella will come to lead a few years down the line as she fights with her husband, the philandering Steve, before noisily making up with him. At the end of the play, although she assures Stella that she is right to reject Blanche's story of rape and has no choice but to stick with Stanley, Eunice nevertheless behaves with sensitivity towards Blanche.

Steve Hubbel

Eunice's husband Steve is one of Stanley's poker buddies. A loutish and lecherous drunk, he may well suggest what Stanley will become in the future. Interestingly, however, when Steve seems uneasy at Blanche's removal to the asylum, it suggests — albeit temporarily — that even Stanley's poker buddies are aware that they are witnessing something terrible. Steve has the very last line of the play, when in the absence of Stanley, who is outside the apartment comforting Stella, he announces that normal service in Elysian Fields has been resumed after Blanche's removal: 'This game is seven-card stud' (p. 90).

Other characters

Pablo

Another poker player, whose ethnic roots show the cultural diversity of Elysian Fields. He, too, is troubled by Blanche's removal.

A Young Man

The young man comes to the Kowalskis' apartment when Blanche is waiting at home for Mitch to collect her for their date. Blanche is attracted to him and kisses him. On the one hand, he is an uneasy

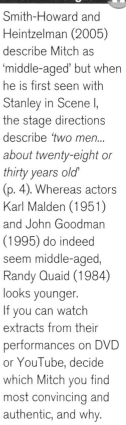

*Pause for **Thought***

Smith-Howard and Heintzelman (2005) describe Mitch as 'middle-aged' but when he is first seen with Stanley in Scene I, the stage directions describe *'two men... about twenty-eight or thirty years old'* (p. 4). Whereas actors Karl Malden (1951) and John Goodman (1995) do indeed seem middle-aged, Randy Quaid (1984) looks younger. If you can watch extracts from their performances on DVD or YouTube, decide which Mitch you find most convincing and authentic, and why.

❰ Top ten *quotation*

reminder of that obsession with very young men which resulted in Blanche being fired from her teaching post; on the other, he evokes the ghost of her tragic husband Allan Grey.

A Negro Woman

Another character who reveals the multicultural nature of the Vieux Carré, the Negro woman appears in the first scene of the play, chatting to Eunice. She is amused by Stanley's unmistakable sexual posturing and when Blanche arrives she offers to fetch Stella from the bowling alley. In Scene X, just before Stanley rapes Blanche, she is seen outside the Kowalskis' apartment, rifling through a prostitute's stolen handbag.

A Mexican Woman

The blind Mexican woman, who sells traditional funeral decorations, alarms Blanche with her eerie cry of *'Flores para los muertos'* — 'flowers for the dead' (p. 74). She functions as a kind of choric figure, further heightening the play's links with classical tragedy.

A Doctor and a Nurse

When he arrives to take Blanche to the asylum the doctor refuses to have Blanche put into a straitjacket and leads her out of the Kowalskis' apartment in a gentlemanlike manner. The nurse's harsh manner serves to highlight his much more sympathetic attitude.

Allan Grey

When Blanche discovered her sensitive and artistic young husband Allan in bed with an older male friend it was the end of her happiness. All three of them got drunk and went off to the Moon Lake Casino. When Blanche told Allan of her disgust at his homosexuality he ran outside and shot himself. Although Allan is never seen on stage he is extremely important; Blanche has never got over her guilt at his death nor found another love to replace him.

Shep Huntleigh

Shep is another character present only in Blanche's memory. A former beau of hers, he comes to represent her last hope of escaping her past.

Context

In classical Greek tragedy the chorus often represented ordinary people as opposed to the great heroes and gods who dominated the action on stage, expressing for the benefit of the audience those ideas and emotions the main characters were unable to voice, such as hidden fears or desires. It is possible to see both the Mexican Woman and the unseen but audible Tamale Vendor as fulfilling aspects of these functions in *Streetcar*.

Task 4

Collate all the textual information that relates to Allan Grey and Shep Huntleigh and assess how they differ from the main flesh-and-blood male characters, Stanley and Mitch.

Form, structure and language

This section is designed to offer you information about the three strands of AO2, the Assessment Objective which requires you to demonstrate detailed critical understanding when analysing the ways in which form, structure and language shape meanings in literary texts. In the next few pages each of these three aspects is dealt with separately in order to clarify the differences between them, but it is important to remember that aspects of form, structure and language often overlap and interact. Therefore this section begins by unifying form, structure and language through an exploration of Williams's own theory of 'plastic theatre'.

Putting it all together: 'plastic theatre'

In his production notes for his first major stage success *The Glass Menagerie* (1944), Williams discussed the need to create an overarching, holistic, organic theatrical experience which aimed to do more than merely reproduce 'reality' by tapping into a wider definition of the 'truth'. He wanted the freedom to utilise the broadest possible range of dramatic techniques and throughout his career he remained true to this conception of a distinctive 'plastic theatre' which incorporates expressionist features to reflect the psychology of his characters — as the Varsouviana does for Blanche — as well as more realistic elements. In a sense, knowing that his plays were about unconventional characters and themes, Williams rightly saw that they needed equally unconventional stage effects; his 'new, plastic theatre', he hoped, would then 'take the place of the exhausted theatre of realistic conventions':

> Expressionism and all other unconventional techniques in drama have only one valid aim, and that is a closer approach to truth. When a play employs unconventional techniques, it is not, or certainly shouldn't be, trying to escape its responsibility of dealing with reality, or interpreting experience, but is actually or should be attempting to find a closer approach, a more penetrating and vivid expression of things as they are. The straight realistic play with its genuine Frigidaire and authentic ice-cubes, its characters who speak exactly as its audience

speaks, corresponds to the academic landscape and has the same virtue of a photographic likeness. Everyone should know nowadays the unimportance of the photographic in art: that truth, life, or reality is an organic thing which the poetic imagination can represent or suggest, in essence, only through transformation, through changing into other forms than those which were merely present in appearance.

For Williams, a play had to do more than merely reflect life as it was; it should try to express some universal insight into the human condition. His modes of dramatic expression are thus many, varied and complex and his concept of 'plastic theatre' places as much value on non-literary and non-verbal elements of drama, such as sound, lighting, movement, setting and design, as it does on dialogue in terms of their ability to convey theme and character. Thus the *Form, structure and language* section which follows will draw attention to many of the non-naturalistic aspects of his work, such as his metaphorical scene descriptions, symbolic use of setting, props, music, sound and lighting, and patterned and poetic dialogue, because Williams saw all these elements as forming part of an organic and overarching dramatic experience. In fact, given his commitment to what might be seen as a kind of total or extreme theatre, worrying about whether to categorise, say, 'imagery' under the heading of form, structure or language completely misses the point. It is far better to think in terms of Williams's own notion of 'plastic theatre', and celebrate the fact that he hit upon a vivid, ambitious and pretty much all-encompassing view of the possibilities of the dramatic medium.

Many features of form, structure and language in the play are explored in other sections of this book, particularly the *Scene summaries and commentaries* on pp. 6–19 and the 'Extended commentary' on pp. 87–89 of this guide.

Form

The essence of a theatrical performance lies in its ephemeral nature, whereas the written text from which it springs is fixed and permanent. When you write about the form, structure and language of a play you must show a keen awareness of the ways in which the dramatic genre works and the specifically theatrical methods used by playwrights to present their ideas. If you remember that the printed version of *Streetcar* is above all a blueprint for performance, and that the play was written to

> For Williams, a play…should try to express some universal insight into the human condition

be seen and heard in the company of others rather than read alone, you are on the right track. Unlike a novel or a poem, a play is not complete in its purely written form; it has to make the transition from page to stage. A theatre audience shares the same physical space as the actors performing; we are separate from the onstage action but eyewitnesses to it in real time and real space. Thus when we read, rather than watch, *Streetcar* we are receiving the text in an incomplete, yet extremely rich and rewarding, form.

If you look at a play written by Shakespeare or one of his contemporaries you will notice a striking lack of detailed stage directions, probably because the playwright himself was available to have some input into the staging of his own work. In the centuries since then, other playwrights have used brief stage directions to tell the actors how to behave, to whom to direct their speech, or what tone of voice to adopt, but in many twentieth-century plays, including those of Williams, the stage directions go way beyond such practical and functional details. Indeed, Williams's precise, rich and often lyrical stage directions are often so thought-provoking that they offer an additional level of enjoyment to the reader which is unavailable to a theatre audience. One of the most characteristic elements of Williams's dramaturgy is the fact that while his characters are presented extremely realistically, his staging is often startlingly non-naturalistic. Part of *Streetcar*'s power stems from watching his penetratingly observed and psychologically convincing characters use heightened and heavily patterned dialogue rich with linguistic motifs as they interact within a consciously stylised onstage world teeming with unusual and symbolic visual and sound effects.

In terms of genre or form, one of the most interesting aspects of *A Streetcar Named Desire* is the various ways in which we might choose to categorise it as, for instance, a twentieth-century American tragedy, a melodrama, or what Williams himself described as a 'memory play'. Generic categories, however, are not fixed but in a constant state of flux. As an active reader, you should aim to locate a range of interesting questions that lurk in the gaps between the apparently overlapping and occasionally contradictory dramatic sub-genres mentioned in this section. One of the most exciting aspects of *Streetcar* is the way in which it seems simultaneously polemical, political, poetic and romantic. In the end, perhaps Williams's artful blurring of literary genres allows us to see how a great writer can be startlingly innovative and original while still conforming to many traditional theatrical practices and conventions.

Twentieth-century American tragedy

> Tragedy is the art form created to confront the most difficult experiences we face: death, loss, injustice, thwarted passion, despair. (Wallace in McEvoy, 2009)

According to the Greek philosopher Aristotle, writing *c*. 330 BC 'the structure of the best tragedy should be not simple but complex and one that represents incidents arousing fear and pity — for that is peculiar to this form of art'. In essence, a tragedy involves the downfall of a great man (the tragic hero) as the result of a reversal of fortune (*peripeteia*) which is the inevitable result of his own actions and involves the concept of *hamartia*, which is usually taken to mean a fatal character flaw. At the play's denouement, the tragic hero gains some insight (*anagnorisis*) into the nature of the human condition, fate or destiny and the will of the gods, while the onlookers are moved to feel pity and terror at what they have seen, thereby achieving a kind of spiritual cleansing in the process (*catharsis*). From the very beginning, it seems, the audience has always been as much a part of the tragic experience as the actors.

In his *Memoirs*, published about 30 years after he had written *Streetcar*, Williams declared:

> I realise how very old-fashioned I am as a dramatist to be so concerned with classic form but this does not embarrass me, since I feel that the absence of form is nearly always, if not always, as dissatisfying to an audience as it is to me. I persist in considering Cat [on a Hot Tin Roof] my best work of the long plays because of its classical unities of time and place and the kingly magnitude of Big Daddy. Yet I seem to contradict myself. I write so often of people with no magnitude, at least on the surface. I write of 'little people'. But are there 'little people'? I sometimes think there are only little conceptions of people. Whatever is living and feeling with intensity is not little and, examined in depth, it would seem to me that most 'little people' are living with that intensity that I can use as a writer.

> Was Blanche a 'little person'? Certainly not. She was a demonic creature, the size of her feeling was too great for her to contain without madness. (Williams, *Memoirs*, 1976)

*Pause for **Thought*** ❚❚

While it is perhaps easier to see Blanche as the tragic protagonist of the play, some readers and audiences might prefer to view Stanley as the hero, and in the earlier scenes he does seem more likeable than Blanche. Where do you stand on this key issue, and what textual evidence would you use to support your point of view?

Tragicomedy, melodrama and soap opera

The one American playwright who is a conspicuous exception to the dichotomy between 'high' and 'low' culture is Tennessee Williams. Williams's South, with its sexual ambivalence, self-delusion, and irrational violence, has become part of our popular mythos, the ambience of countless B-movies and television melodramas. Surely, no play of the American theatre, perhaps no play in English since the time of Shakespeare, has won such praise from both the critics and the populace. (Kolin in R. C. Small, 'A Teacher's Guide to the Signet edition of Tennessee Williams's *A Streetcar Named Desire*', 2004)

As Kolin suggests here, several of Williams's plays have specific qualities which would seem to belong to the 'lowbrow' popular culture genres of melodrama and soap opera rather than the 'highbrow' elite genre of classical tragedy. Melodramas contain sensational incidents, stereotyped characters, exaggerated emotions and simplistic sentiments, whereas soap operas are often intimate, domestic, family-orientated and theoretically realistic. Relatively few texts share common ground with both *Oedipus the King* and *Desperate Housewives*, but several of Williams's key themes — family and sexual politics, greed and betrayal, love and hate, loneliness and death — tap into the perennial concerns important to the audiences who first watched the ancient Greek plays and modern soap addicts alike. Like many of Williams's most memorable characters, Blanche is wrestling with the eternal questions that tortured Oedipus then and now obsess the residents of Wisteria Lane. Who are we? How can we find love? What are we here for?

In another of his great plays, *Cat on a Hot Tin Roof* (1955), Williams blended tragic elements such as the haunting suicide of a tormented homosexual and the terminal cancer of the family patriarch Big Daddy with the comically misplaced belief of his sycophantic and super-fertile daughter-in-law Mae that her gruesome squadron of squabbling brats will net her the family fortune. Similarly, in *A Streetcar Named Desire*, Williams juxtaposes diametrically opposed tragic and comic moods in dramatising rape and madness alongside the domestic squabbling of Blanche and Stanley over her hogging the bathroom and secretly guzzling his whisky. Managing this tragicomic emotional tightrope poses a considerable challenge for actors and audiences alike, yet Williams's skill as a dramatist ensures that the play never descends into cliché or farce as it looks at life in the raw, with all its contradictions and irreconcilabilities.

Williams juxtaposes diametrically opposed tragic and comic moods

Social realist drama

The success of *Streetcar* may have been partly due to the new taste for realism that emerged in postwar America; Stanley and Mitch were fellow soldiers and Blanche slept with many young men from the army base near her home in Laurel. Another realistic aspect of the play is its depiction of the rich cultural and racial background of life in working-class New Orleans. At the denouement, virtually all the characters are on stage, from Blanche and Stella with their aristocratic French ancestry to Polish Stanley, Anglo-Irish Mitch, Mexican Pablo and Steve, whose surname, 'Hubbel', suggests he is of German descent. We have also seen the Mexican Woman and the Negro Woman and heard the black musicians playing their jazz and blues. As Sean McEvoy has noted:

> These are the down-at-heel newcomers, the lower depths working to better themselves the American way, in the troubled pursuit of an(y) American dream. The tragedy in this play...lies not in personal circumstances, but in the lives and the losses of the culture and the society itself. (McEvoy, 2009)

Streetcar is set just after the seismic upheaval of the Second World War, and Williams dramatises a remarkable postwar transformation of America in which the economic contribution of men like Stanley will underpin the dawning of a new age of prosperity. The family unit had been split up and threatened during the war years, but now it was seen as the cornerstone of the nation's recovery. Thus popular culture seemed to endorse traditional gender roles by celebrating the domestic responsibilities of women as homemakers and child carers and closing down the alternative possibilities for women which the war had temporarily offered in the absence of men.

Morality play

In medieval times, morality plays were didactic texts designed to convey a moral lesson; the characters were allegorical archetypes personifying virtues and vices such as 'Mercy' and 'Greed' and the central theme was mankind's struggle against sin. This explicitly Christian form of theatre was meant to teach the audience about abstract concepts such as virtue, vice and repentance.

Clearly there is plenty of sinning in *Streetcar* — in fact, all the so-called seven deadly sins are represented: wrath, avarice, sloth, pride, lust, envy and gluttony. Yet while punishment is meted out to some (but not

*Pause for **Thought***

The 1946 film *The Best Years of Our Lives* is the story of a soldier, a sailor and an airman trying to readjust to civilian life; a huge critical and commercial success, it won seven Academy Awards. Watch a clip over the internet on YouTube — or even see the whole film — to get a sense of the challenges which faced army veterans like Stanley and Mitch after the end of the Second World War.

Task 5

Collect evidence of characters committing each of the seven deadly sins in the play.

all) transgressors, Williams avoids spelling out too schematic a moral message, leaving the moral judgements to his readers and audiences.

Memory play

After the Second World War, partly influenced by the ideas of psychoanalysts like Sigmund Freud and Carl Jung, the idea of the 'memory play' began to influence a new generation of writers. Williams saw all his major works as 'memory plays' that centre on a character undergoing an intense psychological crisis; this incident is so profound it triggers a time-loop trap during which the trauma must be continuously relived until the character comes to terms with it. Thus the action of the play is non-linear and consciously artificial and stylised dramatic techniques are used to suggest a psychological or spiritual 'truth' about the inner life of the main protagonist.

Memory plays seek to convey a symbolic truth as opposed to a naturalistic imitation of reality, and it is fascinating to trace those elements of *Streetcar* which seem to conflict with the notion of a 'realistic' text. Williams's use of the Varsouviana to move Blanche in and out of her memories of the past, for instance, adds immeasurably to the audience's understanding of her character even though it is completely artificial. Unlike the other characters on stage, the audience can hear the music that conjures up her remembered experience; in effect Williams has organised the structural framing in which Blanche's memory of Allan's suicide is embedded to minimise our chances of achieving an objective critical stance and encourage us to empathise with her instead. Thus there are effectively two different types of 'reality' operating here, defined by Felicia Hardison Londré as 'the mingling of objective reality and the subjective reality that is seen through the eyes of Blanche DuBois' (Londré in Roudané, 1997). According to Smith-Howard and Heintzelman (2005), the 1947 Broadway production of *Streetcar* was a 'watershed moment in US theatre history. Essentially, Williams created a new genre in the modern theatre: a heightened naturalism that allows dreams (or nightmares) to coexist with reality.'

Taking it **Further** ▶

Like *Streetcar*, Arthur Miller's *Death of a Salesman* (1949) uses memories to structure the text in a non-linear way. Miller famously challenges the notion that tragedy must focus upon the downfall of a great man: the hero, Willy Loman, is an ordinary 'low' man. Read *Death of a Salesman* and compare and contrast the ways in which Williams and Miller use memory to emphasise their major themes. A Philip Allan Literature Guide is available on *Death of a Salesman*.

Structure

When we talk about the structure of a play, we mean the manner in which it is put together. At A-level you need to understand the ways in

which the structural aspects of a text contribute to and influence our understanding of the text as a whole.

The structure of *Streetcar* is reminiscent of the Russian playwright Anton Chekhov's famous tragicomedy *The Cherry Orchard* (1903). Both plays deal with the annihilation of a genteel rural aristocratic way of life by a rising and brashly confident lower class, begin with an arrival and end with a departure. Moreover, like Chekhov, Williams often uses music and sound effects to heighten dramatic tension.

The arrival of the intruder

Like so many plays, *Streetcar* utilises elements of the classical dramatic structure of crisis and climax. The bare bones of the piece fit numerous other plays in which the on-stage action is set in motion by the arrival of an intruder who invades and disrupts an apparently stable and harmonious world before being expelled, whereupon harmony is (more or less) re-established.

> The bare bones of the piece fit numerous other plays in which the on-stage action is set in motion by the arrival of an intruder who invades and disrupts an apparently stable and harmonious world before being expelled, whereupon harmony is (more or less) re-established

The 11 'scenes'

Unlike most plays, which are divided into acts and scenes, Williams chose to structure *A Streetcar Named Desire* into 11 scenes which trace the development of the relationships between Blanche, Stanley and Stella over the space of a few months. The original stage production placed the two intervals after Scene IV (the poker night) and Scene VI (Blanche's date with Mitch) and it has been suggested that this model effectively divides the play into three sections plus a coda, like this:

- **Scenes I–IV**, set in early May, establish a mood of dark comedy.
- **Scenes V and VI**, set on a swelteringly hot August evening, are melancholic, nostalgic and romantic.
- **Scenes VII–X**, set on the afternoon and evening of Blanche's birthday, 15 September, are powerfully dramatic, climactic and tragic.

Then **Scene XI**, set *'some weeks later'*, presumably in the early autumn, works as a kind of desolate tragic coda.

Movement in time

Whereas the onstage action keeps moving forward until Stanley rapes Blanche, we are also taken backwards in time to Blanche's primal sexual trauma, the discovery of Allan's homosexuality and his subsequent suicide. When Blanche finally describes this event to Mitch, years after it took place, it has entirely changed its 'meaning'; at the time she was shocked, appalled and disgusted, but now she feels guilt, sorrow and remorse. Significantly the play begins in the spring and ends in the 'fall'.

Dramatic climaxes

Another notable structural feature is Williams's decision to end each of the 11 scenes with a vivid punchline, startling tableau or arresting visual image. Note the patterned and repetitive nature of these startlingly dramatic closing moments:

- **Scene I** — Blanche sinks down, puts her head in her hands and announces she is going to be sick.
- **Scene II** — Blanche asks: 'Which way do we — go now — Stella?... The blind are — leading the blind!' (pp. 23–24). The *'blue piano'* and the *'hot trumpet'* are heard.
- **Scene III** — Mitch comforts Blanche who declares: 'Thank you for being so kind! I need kindness now' (p. 34).
- **Scene IV** — Stella embraces Stanley as he grins at Blanche in triumph; the *'blue piano'*, trumpet and drums are heard.
- **Scene V** — Blanche kisses the Young Man and gets rid of him only just in time for Mitch's arrival, whereupon she launches into her Southern belle act to dazzle him.
- **Scene VI** — Blanche and Mitch embrace at the end of their date and Blanche declares: 'Sometimes — there's God — so quickly!' (p. 57).
- **Scene VII** — Blanche realises something has gone badly wrong and when Stella denies anything has happened she shouts: 'You're lying! Something has!' As she and Stella freeze, *'The distant piano goes into a hectic breakdown'* (p. 63).
- **Scene VIII** — Stella goes into labour and as the Varsouviana plays, Blanche sings the Mexican folk-song 'El pain de mais'.
- **Scene IX** — After Mitch attempts to rape her, Blanche screams: 'Fire! Fire! Fire!' and falls to her knees. *'The distant piano is slow and blue'* (p. 75).
- **Scene X** — Stanley attacks Blanche, declaring: 'We've had this date with each other from the beginning!' *'She sinks to her knees. He picks up her inert figure and carries her to the bed. The hot trumpet and drums from the Four Deuces sound loudly'* (p. 81).
- **Scene XI** — Stella weeps in Stanley's arms and as her *'luxurious sobbing'* and his *'sensual murmur'* fade the *'blue piano'* and the

❮ Top ten *quotation*

'*muted trumpet*' are heard as Steve announces: 'This game is seven-card stud' (p. 90).

Interestingly it is in Scene VI — which comes right at the heart of the play as the middle point of the 11 scenes — that Blanche tells Mitch about the suicide of Allan Grey, the defining event of her life. In terms of some of the key moments or events characteristic of classical tragedy, the **crisis** may be identified as Blanche's decision to reveal the truth about her past to Mitch (Scene IX), the **climax** as her rape by Stanley (Scene X) and the **denouement** her removal to the asylum (Scene XI). Above all, however, it is important to note that the episodic, impressionistic structure of the text allows Williams to reveal crucial snippets of information about Blanche's past scene by scene, thus heightening the dramatic tension. *Streetcar*'s structure is thus much looser than that of *Cat on a Hot Tin Roof*, which Williams felt was his most skilfully constructed play in observing the unities of time, place and action. The on-stage action of *Cat on a Hot Tin Roof* plays out in real time, as a highly dysfunctional family goes into meltdown, squabbling over a $10 million fortune and '28,000 acres of the richest land this side of the valley Nile'.

Context

According to Aristotle, the three classical *unities* (rules for drama) are *unity of action*: a play should track one main plot, with no (or few) subplots; *unity of place*: the action should take place in one location; and *unity of time*: the action should take place within a single day.

Aspects of setting and staging

In purely theatrical terms, Williams's radical rethinking of how to use the stage space was seen as particularly innovative when the play was first performed. In allowing the audience to witness the events taking place both in the Kowalskis' small cramped flat and the pulsing urban jungle of the Vieux Carré outside, he juxtaposed the realistic and the symbolic in a way which came to be seen as one of his signature dramatic techniques. A vast number of sound and lighting cues serve to heighten the audience's awareness of the psychological states of the characters, while Williams's famously poetic and metaphorical stage directions go well beyond 'exit stage left' to function as an omniscient narrative viewpoint very unusual in drama. Thus *Streetcar*, like most of his other plays, is almost as rewarding to encounter as a reader as to experience in performance.

According to Thomas Adler:

> **Williams fully utilized the stylistic possibilities of the stage...to break away from the language-bound realistic drama of the nineteenth century....This new type of play would not only admit but insist that the language of drama involves more than just words; it would acknowledge the**

stage symbols and the scenic images that speak to the audience as powerfully as what issues from the mouths of the characters. (Adler in Small, 2004)

In *Streetcar* the cramped flat is the arena for combat as Blanche and Stanley fight for physical space and emotional territory with all their associated connotations of invasion and defence, attraction and repulsion. Because Blanche has to sleep on a collapsible put-you-up camp bed it is suggested from the outset that she will be merely passing through Elysian Fields on her journey towards her final destination, Cemeteries; meanwhile the fact that her sleeping quarters are only cordoned off by a flimsy curtain represents her ominous lack of security and protection when living under Stanley's roof.

Setting and staging: the interior and the exterior

The fact that the street outside the Kowalskis' cramped apartment is also visible to the audience implies that the home offers scant protection from the wider world. Other places mentioned but never seen remind us of further aspects of the characters' lives — the bowling alley and the Four Deuces provide an index for Stanley's macho working-class world just as Belle Reve, the Moon Lake Casino and the Flamingo Hotel are the staging posts for Blanche's downfall. The interface between these inside and outside spaces suggests the apartment is a liminal or threshold place rather than a safe haven; just before Stanley rapes Blanche the back wall of the apartment becomes transparent, revealing the brutal and animalistic violence occurring on the street which prefigures the violation about to happen inside.

Metatheatre

Metatheatre is a self-conscious awareness in a play of its status as a theatrical performance. Such awareness can work through the persistent use of theatrical images, metaphors, or through more overt structural devices such as a 'play within the play'. Blanche is from the start a woman in disguise, a woman who orchestrates a range of theatrical performances to cover up the reality she cannot bear to face. In *A Streetcar Named Desire* there are a number of important metatheatrical references, images and elements that contribute to the overall structural cohesion of the text:

- When Blanche first arrives at Elysian Fields, she is described as *'daintily dressed in a white suit with a fluffy bodice, necklace and*

Context

In *Cat on a Hot Tin Roof*, Williams describes the Pollitt mansion as *'Victorian with a touch of the Far East'*, thus neatly encapsulating that play's uneasy juxtaposition of foreign, erotic and exotic elements and stifling conservative morality.

Context

Shakespeare's *Hamlet* (1606) contains the most famous example of a 'play-within-a-play' ever written. Hamlet asks some strolling players to perform a play he calls 'The Mousetrap' in order to expose his uncle's murder of Hamlet's father, telling himself 'the play's the thing,/ Wherein I'll catch the conscience of the king'. In *Streetcar*, the tableau of the prostitute, the drunk and the Negro woman dramatises a minor crime while foreshadowing (as opposed to mirroring) a worse one.

earrings of pearl, white gloves and hat, looking as if she were arriving at a summer tea or cocktail party in the garden district' (p. 5). She is, in other words, inappropriately costumed for this context.

Top ten *quotation*❯

- Blanche's trunk of clothes may be seen as a kind of dressing-up box in which she stores the costumes she needs in order to perform her chosen roles. Stanley sees this clearly, asking Stella: 'What is this sister of yours, a deep-sea diver who brings up sunken treasures? Or is she the champion safe-cracker of all time?' (p. 18). Cruelly but accurately, Stanley sums up her life in Laurel as 'the same old lines, same old act, same old hooey' (p. 60). Later he taunts her with her efforts to create an appropriate 'setting' in which to perform: 'You come in here and sprinkle the place with powder and spray perfume and cover the light-bulb with a paper lantern, and lo and behold the place has turned into Egypt and you are the Queen of the Nile!' (p. 79).

- Mitch is Blanche's admiring audience in Scene III as she uses music and choreography to create her illusions and maintains her performance throughout Scenes V and VI. Once Stanley has told Mitch about Blanche's past, it is sheer outrage at the gap between the ladylike spinster schoolmarm role she has been playing all summer for his benefit and the sordid truth about the Flamingo Hotel that provokes him to violence in Scene IX.

- In Scene I Stanley removes his vest in front of Blanche, which is clearly inappropriate as well as offering an implied sexual threat, while his gaudy bowling shirt signals his brash and competitive nature. When he appears wearing the silk pyjamas he bought for his wedding night with Stella, his costume seems to suggest that his rape of her sister is predestined.

- At the start of Scene X Blanche is described as having *'decked herself out in a somewhat soiled and crumpled white satin evening gown and a pair of scuffed silver slippers... she is placing the rhinestone tiara on her head before the mirror of the dressing-table and murmuring excitedly as if to a group of spectral admirers'* (p. 75). In effect she is presented as an actress putting the final touches to her costume before going on stage.

- Williams makes use of a non-naturalistic tableau or mini 'play within a play' with the interpolated vignette of the prostitute, the drunk and the Negro Woman in Scene X.

- In Scene XI Blanche is dressed first in a *'red satin robe'* (p. 83), which connotes sexuality, before changing into a jacket of 'Della Robbia blue. The blue of the robe in the old Madonna pictures' (p. 84). Symbolically she may be seen as shedding the costume (and hence the role) of the 'scarlet woman' here and adopting instead the persona of the Holy Virgin. As she talks to Stella and Eunice, she is hidden behind the 'portières' — full-length curtains which serve to divide the living space. In effect, Blanche is seen to be waiting for the curtain to rise on her final performance in the Kowalskis' apartment.

Vivien Leigh and Marlon Brando in Elia Kazan's film version of 1951

Task 6

There are frequent references to acting and performance throughout the play, such as 'make-believe' and 'putting on an act'. Working either on your own or with a partner, collect as many other instances of metatheatre as possible and analyse the ways in which this technique may shed light on Williams's themes and characters.

Binary opposites

The concept of binary opposites stems from the work of the French intellectuals Claude Lévi-Strauss (1908–2009) and Roland Barthes (1915–80), who were closely associated with the theory of structuralism.

In terms of literary theory, structuralists argue that since the meaning of a word is not actually contained in its name, we tend to construct its meaning by relating each word to its opposite. They characterise words as symbols which signify society's ideas and suggest that meaning emerges from the 'gap' between two opposing concepts; thus in order to grasp an idea such as masculinity, we refer to its binary opposite, femininity. Layers of inferential meaning can emerge when a writer consciously structures a text using core oppositions and patterns like this, and in *Streetcar* Williams makes frequent use of this technique by inviting his readers and audiences to consider such dichotomies, particularly as embodied by Stanley and Blanche:

- masculinity and femininity
- birth and death
- regeneration and decay

Context

Structuralism has been defined as the search for the underlying patterns of thought in all aspects of human life; it involves comparing the relationships between elements in any given system.

- materialism and idealism
- physicality and spirituality
- new and old
- present and past
- fertility and sterility
- bold colour and white light

Williams often places similar or contrasting ideas or concepts close together to shed light on them both. Consider Williams's reasons for using the structural techniques of **juxtapositioning**, **patterning** and **doubling** in the following examples:

- The first half of the play is dominated by Stanley, who generally gets most sympathy from the audience here; this is reversed in the latter stages as we come to transfer our sympathies to Blanche.
- Blanche queens it over the bathroom; Stanley's poker buddies throw him into the shower to sober up.
- Blanche sings 'Paper Moon' in the bathroom while Stanley tells Stella the truth about her sister's life behind Blanche's back.
- Blanche discusses Hawthorne, Whitman, Poe and Browning with Mitch (Scene III) while Stella reads 'a book of coloured comics' in Scene IV just before Blanche tries to appeal to her to recognise 'art', 'poetry' and 'music' as necessary for a civilised life.
- Stanley removes his vest in front of Blanche while she asks him to zip up the back of her dress.
- Stanley rifles through Blanche's trunk; she steals his whisky and hides the evidence.
- The choric figures darken; first we hear the tamale seller with his 'red hots'; later it is the Mexican woman selling her flowers for the dead.
- Both Stanley and Blanche are shown as hardened heavy drinkers; but he is free to drink with his poker buddies in public, the social mores of the genteel Old South mean she has to lie about her drinking and keep it secret.

Foreshadowing

Foreshadowing is a way of providing structural cohesion by dropping hints to the audience which can help them to predict future events. Williams makes much use of this technique:

Task 7

Analyse Williams's purpose in establishing Blanche as a practised drinker who is not above sneaking Stanley's whisky behind his back in Scene I; he comments 'Liquor goes fast in hot weather' (p. 14) as he *holds the bottle to the light to observe its depletion'*. What is the effect on the audience here?

- In Scene I, Stanley throws a package of meat for Stella to catch, which Eunice and the Negro woman find highly amusing; they have clearly decoded the sexual innuendo behind his macho gesture. In hurling the meat Stanley signals his sexual domination over her and in catching it, Stella reveals the depth of her sexual obsession with him.

- Stanley's metaphorical rape of Blanche's trunk, jewellery and love-letters, plus Mitch's botched assault on her, prefigure the climax of the play.

- Stanley's 'breakdown' during the poker night, which involves him being overwhelmed against his will by his friends, foreshadows Blanche's breakdown and forcible restraint before she is taken to the asylum.

- Blanche's kissing the Young Man foreshadows the revelation that she was sacked for seducing her pupil.

Language

Task 8

In Scene II Blanche is heard singing the sentimental ballad 'From the land of the sky blue water'. The lyrics can be found at **http://en.wikipedia.org** by searching on 'land sky blue water'.

Analyse how these melancholy words may capture something of Blanche's ambivalent position in the Kowalskis' apartment and foreshadow the play's dramatic climax.

Language in *A Streetcar Named Desire* taps into a wide range of dramatic effects. Thus, for example, the following section discusses stage directions — which are obviously not part of the experience of an audience in the theatre in written form — in order to stress that 'language' in this play needs to be seen as more than simply words or dialogue, but as an integral part of Williams's overarching 'plastic theatre' experience.

The play's title

Williams was a genius at signalling the central theme of a text with an evocative metaphorical title which gets straight to the heart of things (see also *Cat on a Hot Tin Roof*) but if the brilliantly sleazy *A Streetcar Named Desire* is not the greatest title ever, it is hard to think of many that can rival it. As Felicia Hardison Londré notes, 'the mundane concreteness of "streetcar" and the abstract quality of aspiration evoked in "desire" point to the many antinomies — thematic, symbolic, and imagistic oppositions — imbedded throughout the play' (Londré in Roudané, 1997). Moreover, the fact that there really were streetcars called Desire and Cemeteries rattling through New Orleans reinforces the real-life context and setting of the play as well as drawing attention to Blanche's fatal journey via Elysian Fields to her symbolic 'death' in the asylum.

Although he had apparently had *A Streetcar Named Desire* in mind all along, Williams did consider some other potential titles for the play. In 1945 he wrote to his agent, Audrey Wood: 'I have been buried in work the last week or so and am about 55 or 60 pages into the first draft of a play which I am trying to design for [famous actress Katharine] Cornell. At the moment it has four different titles, *The Moth*, *The Poker Night*, *The Primary Colors*, or Blanche's *Chair in the Moon*. It is about two sisters, the remains of a fallen Southern family. The younger, Stella, has accepted the situation, married beneath her socially and moved to a Southern city with her coarsely attractive, plebeian mate. But Blanche (the Cornell part) has remained at Belle-reve, the home place in ruins, and struggles for five years to maintain the old order' (Williams, *Notebooks*, 2006).

Task 9

Consider the possible significance of Williams's four rejected titles and suggest which of the play's themes each seems to encapsulate.

Images, motifs and symbols

Writers often use related language patterns and clusters to infuse certain characters with particular associations, evoke a specific mood or atmosphere, or draw attention to a particularly significant theme. In *Streetcar* Williams uses recurring images, motifs and symbols to create a sense of dramatic and structural coherence and while his symbolism is often verbal (which is why this section has been placed under the AO2 strand of 'language') it is important to remember that he interweaves and reinforces these linguistic images with powerfully vivid aural and visual effects. Thus it is important to think about how the overarching effects of Williams's highly wrought, complex range of images, motifs and symbols enrich the unique atmosphere of the play.

Some of *Streetcar*'s most powerful visual, aural and verbal motifs and symbols are listed here:

- **The coke stain on Blanche's white dress**, which symbolises her tarnished past.
- **Blanche's frequent baths**, which suggest her wish to cleanse herself.
- **The Chinese paper lantern**, which represents Blanche's wish to disguise reality and substitute 'magic'.
- **The streetcar's journey**, which connotes sexual passion.
- **Desire and Cemeteries**, which connote Blanche's fatal journey and explicitly link sex and death in terms of two types of love characterised by Freud as *eros* (the desire for life) and *thanatos* (the longing for oblivion and death).
- **The Varsouviana**, which represents the death of Allan Grey.

- **The blue piano**, which evokes the earthy multicultural atmosphere of the Vieux Carré.
- **Blanche and Stanley** as symbolic archetypes reflecting a wider cultural debate about the nature of the Old South and the new postwar America.

Animals

- Blanche is described as having something about her that suggests a 'moth' (p. 5).
- Stella describes Stanley to Blanche as of a 'different species' (p. 10).
- Blanche asks Stella if Mitch is a 'wolf' (p. 27).
- After Stanley throws the radio out of the window Stella yells: 'Drunk — drunk — animal thing, you!' (p. 31).
- When he calls for Stella, Stanley is described as *throw[ing] back his head like a baying hound'* (p. 33).
- When they make up after their fight Stanley and Stella are said to *'come together with low animal moans'* (p. 33).
- In her set-piece speech to Stella, Blanche describes Stanley as 'bestial', 'like an animal' and 'ape-like' (pp. 40–41).
- Stanley mocks Blanche as she sings in the bathroom as 'canary-bird' (p. 59, 63).
- Stella is disgusted by Stanley's table manners and calls him a 'pig' (p. 65).
- Mitch accuses Blanche of 'lapping it up all summer like a wild-cat!' (p. 71).
- Blanche renames the Flamingo Hotel the 'Tarantula Arms' and describes herself as 'a big spider! That's where I brought my victims' (p. 73).
- Blanche talks of 'casting her pearls before swine' to Stanley (p. 78).
- The outside scene in the Vieux Carré is described as a 'jungle' and *'inhuman voices like cries in a jungle'* are heard (p. 79).
- Stanley 'springs' at Blanche, calling her 'Tiger — tiger!' in excitement as she tries to fight him off (p. 81).
- Eunice accuses the men of 'making pigs of yourselves' (p. 82).
- Blanche wants to wear a brooch shaped like a 'seahorse' (p. 82) for her imaginary cruise with Shep Huntleigh.
- As Blanche is about to be taken to the asylum, *'cries and noises of the jungle'* are heard (p. 87).

Task **10**

Analyse these key imagery clusters and assess the ways in which they serve to highlight Williams's themes. If you work with other students here you might allocate one section to each group. Each group might produce a PowerPoint or poster that logs and analyses such instances to present to the rest of the class.

- When Blanche screams in fear as Stanley tears the lantern down, *'the men spring to their feet'* (pp. 87–88).
- As the doctor calms Blanche, *'the inhuman cries and noises die out'* (p. 89).
- Stella *'sobs with inhuman abandon'* after Blanche has been taken away (p. 89).

Fire, redness, blood and heat

- Blanche uses the word 'bleeding' to describe the suffering of the dying at Belle Reve (p. 12).
- Blanche emerges from the bathroom *'in a red satin robe'* (p. 18).
- After Stanley snatches her love-letters from Allan Grey, Blanche declares 'I'll burn them!' (p. 22).
- Blanche tells Stella that Stanley is 'what we need to mix with our blood now that we've lost Belle Reve' (p. 23).
- The Mexican tamale vendor calls out 'red hots!' (p. 23).
- Stanley complains 'Goddamn, it's hot in here with the steam from the bathroom' (p. 67).
- Blanche shouts 'Fire! Fire! Fire!' to scare Mitch away (p. 75).
- Stanley tells Blanche it is 'a red letter night for us both' (p. 77).
- Blanche appears with *'a tragic radiance in her red satin robe following the sculptural lines of her body'* (p. 83).

Water, sea and rain

- Blanche sings 'From the land of the sky blue water/They brought a captive maid' (p. 16).
- Stanley asks 'What is this sister of yours, a deep-sea diver who brings up sunken treasures?' (p. 18).
- Stanley's card game is called 'Spit in the Ocean' (p. 28).
- After his drunken rage on poker night, Stanley says 'I want water' and is thrown into the shower by Mitch (p. 32).
- Blanche tells Stella she has sought protection under 'leaky roof[s]... because it was storm — all storm' (p. 45).
- Blanche asks the Young Man, 'Don't you just love these long rainy afternoons' (p. 48).
- Blanche tells Mitch about Allan's suicide and the sight of his dead body, 'the terrible thing at the edge of the lake' (p. 57).
- Stanley tells Stella that when Blanche had to leave Laurel she was 'washed up like poison' (p. 60).

- Blanche declares after one of her many baths, 'Oh, I feel so good after my long, hot bath, I feel so good and cool and — rested!' (p. 63).

- Blanche fantasises about 'taking a swim, a moonlight swim at the old rock-quarry…only you've got to be careful to dive where the deep pool is — if you hit a rock you don't come up until tomorrow' (p. 75).

- Blanche tells Stanley she is going on 'a cruise of the Caribbean on a yacht' with Shep Huntleigh (p. 76).

- Stanley foams up the beer bottle and holds it over his head saying to Blanche, 'Ha-ha! Rain from heaven!…Shall we bury the hatchet and make it a loving-cup?' (p. 77).

- Blanche asks if the grapes are 'washed'. She declares, 'I can smell the sea air…when I die, I'm going to die on the sea…And I'll be buried at sea sewn up in a clean white sack and dropped overboard…into an ocean as blue as my first lover's eyes!' (pp. 84–85).

Light

- Blanche's *'delicate beauty must avoid a strong light'* (p. 5).

- Stella tells Blanche she is 'standing in the light' and is visible through the curtains to the poker players (p. 27).

- Blanche asks Mitch to place an 'adorable little coloured paper lantern' over the bare bulb in the bedroom (p. 30).

- Blanche asks the Young Man to light her cigarette (p. 48).

- Blanche tells Mitch 'I want to create — *joie de vivre*! I'm lighting a candle' (p. 52).

- Blanche tells Mitch being in love with Allan Grey was like turning on 'a blinding light' but that since his death 'the searchlight which had been turned on the world was turned off again and never for one moment since has there been any light that's stronger than this — kitchen — candle' (pp. 56–57).

- Stella lights the candles on Blanche's birthday cake (p. 66).

- Stanley describes making love with Stella as getting 'them coloured lights going' (p. 68).

- Mitch forces Blanche into the light and stares at her as she 'cries out and covers her face' (p. 72).

- As Blanche is being taken to the asylum, Stanley rips down her paper lantern *'and extends it towards her. She cries out as if the lantern was herself'* (p. 87).

❮ Top ten *quotation*

Pause for Thought ⏸

A classic episode of *The Simpsons*, 'A Streetcar Named Marge' (excerpts are on YouTube), contains humour deriving from Stanley's dialogue, such as Ned Flanders's Stanley screeching: 'STELLA! STELLA!/Can't you hear me yell-a/You're putting me through hell-a/STELLA! STELLA!'

Which aspects of Williams's form, structure, language and themes stand out to you as distinctive enough to be spoofed on a mainstream television comedy series?

Task 11

Collect examples of dialogue that you find particularly effective and analyse how they enhance your understanding of Williams's characters and themes.

Dialogue

Williams is famous for the way he brings his hauntingly memorable characters to life through dialogue which can be realistic, vivid, poetic, tragic, comic — and sometimes all of the above. In Shakespeare's day, blank verse was the usual form of language for characters of a high social rank while common characters often spoke in prose; in *Streetcar*, Blanche's dreamy, educated, high-register language, which incorporates literary references and French and Spanish vocabulary, is a world away from Stanley's colloquial working-class demotic argot. Blanche is an English teacher, so literature is obviously part and parcel of her stock-in-trade, but Williams carefully chooses her authors and references to add extra layers of meaning. Her ability to summon up apt literary allusions and references makes her speech sound very different from that of Stella, who, like Stanley, is much more literal.

Williams's lyrical and beautiful dialogue is one of his most characteristic qualities as a dramatist, although one which he came to feel left him 'dated' later in his career. In the mid-1960s, when his reputation was in decline, he wrote:

> **My great bête noir[e] as a writer has been a tendency…to poeticize…and that's why I suppose I've written so many Southern heroines. They have the tendency to gild the lily, and they speak in a rather florid style which seems to suit me because I write out of emotion, and I get carried away by emotion. (Williams, 2006)**

In *Streetcar*, however, when he was at the peak of his dramatic powers, his dialogue was (and still is) seen as one of the greatest strengths of the play. The critic Alfred Uhry has suggested that A Streetcar Named Desire 'contains the finest dialogue ever written for an American play'.

The four main characters are very clearly differentiated by their dialogue. Blanche's language includes artificial, affected and stylised elements which Stanley scorns as 'phoney', and Williams gives her symbolic songs to sing. Stanley's language is direct, aggressive, colloquial, sometimes crude and often downright funny. Stella's language is characteristically straightforward, prosaic, sensible and down-to-earth, while Mitch's dialogue is an oddly touching mixture of the naively and comically simplistic and the lyrically tender.

Contexts

This section is designed to offer you an insight into the influence
of some significant contexts in which *A Streetcar Named Desire* was
written and has been performed and received. AO4, remember, requires
demonstration of an understanding of the significance of contexts of
production and reception. Such contextual material should, however,
be used with caution. Reference to contexts is only valuable when it
genuinely informs a reading of the text. Contextual material which is
clumsily introduced or 'bolted on' to an argument will contribute very
little to the argument.

Biographical context

Thomas Lanier Williams was born in Mississippi in 1911, to a particularly
ill-matched couple. Hard-drinking travelling salesman Cornelius Coffin
Williams (C.C.) had little in common with his highly strung, snobbish
wife Edwina, the daughter of a clergyman, and they were at odds
for most of their married life. The middle child of three, 'Tom' was
extremely close to his mother and his sister, Rose, and remained on
friendly terms with his younger brother, Dakin, who was C.C.'s favourite,
but he feared and hated his abusive, bullying father. This unhappy and
dysfunctional family moved around a lot during his childhood and he
was restless and unsettled throughout his adult life.

Williams grew into a shy, gentle, artistic young man. After some early
success in publishing short stories and articles he studied journalism
at the University of Missouri where he was nicknamed 'Tennessee' by
his fellow students on account of his Southern birth. Unfortunately C.C.
forced him to withdraw from his course and get a job as a clerk at the
shoe factory where he himself worked, and after three years of this
drudgery, Williams had a nervous breakdown. Meanwhile his beloved
sister was showing signs of severe mental illness and was diagnosed
with dementia praecox (an early name for schizophrenia) at the age of
just 18. Rose was subjected to an extreme and radical form of primitive
brain surgery (a pre-frontal lobotomy) and then consigned to a mental
institution until her death in 1996. Margaret Bradham Thornton suggests
that *'the shadow of what happened to Rose* stayed with [him]; she would

Context

Of Rose's decline into
madness Williams
(2006) wrote: 'We
have had no deaths in
our family but slowly
by degrees something
was happening much
uglier and more terrible
than death.' This
comment — reminiscent
of the Gothic horrors
Blanche witnessed at
Belle Reve — suggests
that for Williams, who
had once thought of
ending *Streetcar* with
his heroine throwing
herself under a train, her
removal to the county
asylum may have been
even worse.

be the model for more than fifteen characters, and Williams would give her name to many others' (Williams, 2006).

Although traumatised with guilt at what he saw as his failure to protect Rose, after transferring to the University of Iowa Williams finally graduated in 1938 at the age of 27. For the next few years he lived a bohemian and peripatetic existence while continuing to work on his short stories and plays. Finally, in 1944, *The Glass Menagerie* opened to rave reviews and made him an overnight theatrical sensation, followed three years later by the play for which he will always be remembered, the multi-award-winning *A Streetcar Named Desire*. In the decade or so after *Streetcar*, Williams maintained a tremendous work rate, writing other major plays such as *The Rose Tattoo* (1951), *Cat on a Hot Tin Roof* (1955) and *Sweet Bird of Youth* (1959). Unfortunately, as Margaret Bradham Thornton puts it, '[this] prodigious output took its toll on Williams, and while his plays were winning awards and being made into films…Williams was losing his way' (Williams, 2006). Moreover despite his professional success, his private life was always at least bordering on the chaotic and disastrous. He had a long relationship with his secretary Frank Merlo (who loyally supported Williams through frequent bouts of clinical depression) when homosexuality was still considered immoral and shocking by mainstream society, but following Merlo's death in 1963, his life seemed to spiral out of control.

Between 1959 and 1979, although he wrote 15 new plays as well as poetry, a novel and some short stories, only one work, *The Night of the Iguana* (1961) was well received, and his critical reputation went into a sharp decline which lasted until his death. At the same time his depression worsened and in 1969 his brother Dakin had to have him temporarily committed to a psychiatric hospital due to his alcoholism and drug addiction. By the time of his lonely death in a New York hotel room in 1983, the glory days were long behind him.

In his fascinating essay 'Person-to-Person', Williams wrote:

> **I still find it somehow easier to 'level with' crowds of strangers in the hushed twilight of orchestra and balcony sections of theatres than with individuals across a table from me. Their being strangers somehow makes them more familiar and more approachable, easier to talk to.**
> **(Williams, *Cat on a Hot Tin Roof and Other Plays*, 1976)**

Given this statement, although we must be careful not to assume that any text is a simplistic reworking of the writer's own personal experience, it is at least worth discussing how far his greatest and most unforgettable characters — Blanche and Stanley in *Streetcar*, Brick, Big

---

Pause for *Thought* ⏸

The poet Ted Hughes (1930–98) declared: 'Every work of art stems from a wound in the soul of the artist…Art is a psychological component of the auto-immune system that gives expression to the healing process. That is why great works of art make us feel good.' Think about the extent to which this might be true of Williams's work.

Daddy and Maggie in *Cat on a Hot Tin Roof,* and Amanda, Tom and Laura in *The Glass Menagerie,* for instance — may be seen to reflect aspects of his mother, father, sister and even himself. For many of his audiences, readers and critics, it is endlessly fascinating to speculate about the interplay between Williams's life and art, with homosexuality, mental illness, alcoholism, drug addiction, domestic violence and family dysfunction forming so large a part of his personal truth as well as his fictional world.

Historical, social and cultural contexts

The American Century and American Dream

It was Henry Luce, the influential publisher of *Life* magazine, who coined the phrase 'the American Century' to encapsulate what many people saw as the United States' duty to use its unparalleled power and influence for the greater good of the world. Writing in 1941, Luce urged his fellow Americans to enter the Second World War and back the Allies rather than remain isolated, as they had done for most of the First World War. He argued:

> **Throughout the 17th century and the 18th century and the 19th century, this continent teemed with manifold projects and magnificent purposes. Above them all and weaving them all together into the most exciting flag of all the world and of all history was the triumphal purpose of freedom. It is in this spirit that all of us are called, each to his own measure of capacity, and each in the widest horizon of his vision, to create the first great American Century.**

This idealistic global aspiration can be seen as allied with another equally powerful myth which played out in a more domestic context: the notion of 'the American Dream'. This concept grew out of the Declaration of Independence (4 July 1776) in which the Founding Fathers of America set out their vision in the justification for breaking away from British rule:

> We hold these Truths to be self-evident that all men are
> created equal, that they are endowed, by their Creator,
> with certain unalienable Rights, that among these are Life,
> Liberty and the Pursuit of Happiness.

James Truslow Adams, who coined the phrase in 1931, suggested:

> [The American Dream] that has lured tens of millions of
> all nations to our shores in the past century has not been
> a dream of material plenty, though that has doubtlessly
> counted heavily. It has been a dream of being able to grow
> to fullest development as a man and woman, unhampered
> by the barriers which had slowly been erected in the older
> civilizations, unrepressed by social orders which had
> developed for the benefit of classes rather than for the
> simple human being of any and every class.

America has often portrayed itself as a 'melting pot' nation which
welcomes immigrants of all races and religions to a new life of freedom
and opportunity. Often escaping from poverty, oppression and conflict,
America seemed a blank slate upon which they could create their vision
of a land of freedom and opportunity where success depended not on
birth or privilege but on hard work and courage. This idealistic vision is
encapsulated in the words of Emma Lazarus (1849–87), inscribed on the
pedestal of the Statue of Liberty, in which the New World of America
addresses the old:

> Give me your tired, your poor,
> Your huddled masses yearning to breathe free
> The wretched refuse of your teeming shore.
> Send these, the homeless, tempest-tossed to me,
> I lift my lamp beside the golden door!

In summary, then, 'the American Century' and 'the American Dream'
were concepts fully rooted in the cultural landscape of the postwar era.
The former represented the United States as a kind of Good Samaritan
helping other countries to achieve democracy, progress and economic
security, while the latter was a way of uniting the various different
groups of immigrants who came to the USA in the nineteenth and early
twentieth centuries to create a cohesive national ethos.

In time, however, as things began to seem rather less glorious and
more materialistic, many writers became preoccupied with showing
how the American Dream had died — or even that it had only ever
been an illusion in the first place. Once 'life, liberty and the pursuit of

happiness' can be used to justify the actions of people — like Stanley Kowalski — who are set on claiming their slice of the action at any price, it seemed to many writers high time to question whether this mythic totem of popular culture did little more than make people increasingly unhappy, competitive and insecure. In suggesting that society was basically a level playing field, the responsibility for personal success or failure fell squarely upon the individual, and in a supposed meritocracy it can be much harder to blame one's lack of success on other people.

Thus it is in their relentless and painful probing of the gap between the underpinning cultural tradition of twentieth-century America and what they saw as the essential truth of the matter that the great tragic dramatists Tennessee Williams, Arthur Miller and Eugene O'Neill found their essential theme; they set out to question the cultural values which the vast majority of their contemporaries held dear. As Sean McEvoy has written:

> ...tragedy is the art form that knows that the world is not ideal. Because the heart of American culture is the idea that 'all are created equal', old ideas of tragic drama as a form that relies on the upper class or the monarchy for its tragic heroes is not appropriate for telling the American tragedy. (McEvoy, 2009)

The American South and New Orleans

The 'American South' is used more an expression of an entire way of life than as a geographical location. Even today, the South has its own distinctive way of life and its culture, food, literature and music have influenced the rest of the country immensely. Always a cultural melting pot, the South's rich mix of Native Americans, European settlers and imported African slaves has had a major impact upon its history and collective psyche.

During the American Civil War (1861–65), the Southern 'Confederate' states (including Mississippi, Alabama, Georgia, Louisiana, Texas, Virginia and Tennessee) fought against the mainly Northern 'Union' states to defend their right to keep slaves. After the heavy defeat of the South, slavery was officially abolished throughout America in 1865 and from then on the industrialised North grew inexorably more powerful, both politically and economically, than the still largely agricultural South.

Taking it Further ➤

Other archetypal American Dream texts which you might enjoy comparing with *Streetcar* include F. Scott Fitzgerald's *The Great Gatsby* (1925), John Steinbeck's *Of Mice and Men* (1937), and Miller's plays *All My Sons (1947)* and *Death of a Salesman* (1949).

Context

Abraham Lincoln (1809–65) became president of the USA in 1861. Knowing that his Republican Party was anti-slavery, the Southern slave-owning states broke away from the Union. Lincoln steered his country through the Civil War, but six days after the South's final surrender he was assassinated by the fanatical Southern actor John Wilkes Booth.

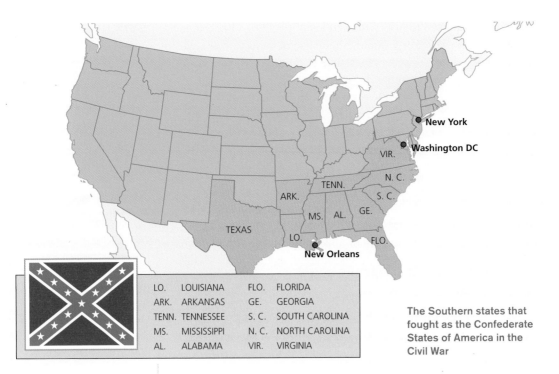

LO.	LOUISIANA	FLO.	FLORIDA
ARK.	ARKANSAS	GE.	GEORGIA
TENN.	TENNESSEE	S. C.	SOUTH CAROLINA
MS.	MISSISSIPPI	N. C.	NORTH CAROLINA
AL.	ALABAMA	VIR.	VIRGINIA

The Southern states that fought as the Confederate States of America in the Civil War

ante-bellum

(from Latin before the war) often used of the Old South prior to the defining event of the American Civil War

Context

After Hurricane Katrina (2005), when 80% of the city's 225,000 inhabitants had to be evacuated when the city flooded, there was a feeling that the federal government would have acted more decisively if rich white northerners had been affected rather than poor, mainly black Southerners.

After the Civil War, many white Southerners bought into an enduring nostalgic mythic representation of the South in its **ante-bellum** heyday as a haven of peace, prosperity and chivalrous gallantry. For black Southerners the Old South was a completely different story. In *Streetcar*, which is set more than 80 years after the end of the Civil War, it is still possible to see that the seeds of the events that lead to Blanche's tragic downfall were sown way back in time when the degenerate aristocratic DuBois began to drink, whore and gamble away Belle Reve, which we can be sure was anything but a beautiful dream for the slaves who worked the plantation.

New Orleans, the city in which Blanche found herself a stranger, is world famous for its multicultural and multilingual heritage and as the birthplace of jazz, but all the beautiful Spanish-style architecture, dazzling Mardi Gras parades and delicious soul food cannot obscure the extreme poverty in which many of its inhabitants live even today. In some people's eyes, 'the Big Easy' should never have been built where it was; the climate is hot and humid, and because it is surrounded by water on three sides, flooding is a constant risk.

In *Streetcar*, Williams dramatises a brutal culture clash between the New Orleans industrial worker and his aristocratic intellectual rival. Enraged and intimidated by the old-fashioned Southern values Blanche embodies,

Stanley determines — albeit unconsciously at first — to destroy the threat she poses to his brave new world. Stella is presented as caught between her loyalty to the 'beautiful dream' of the past, symbolised by Blanche and their lost childhood home in the countryside, and the brash and thrilling immediacy of her new life in the big city of New Orleans. Once upon a time Blanche might have defined herself solely in terms of her status as a ladylike Southerner and even after her arrival in New Orleans' Vieux Carré she persists in keeping up this act because it is so much less painful than facing the truth about her penniless, hard-drinking, promiscuous existence. But Stanley — go-getting, practical, down-to-earth and materialistic — will have none of it. Stella's baby is born on the very night he brutally rapes Blanche and tips her into outright madness; Stella's decision to stay with the father of her child and allow her sister to be committed to a mental asylum may symbolise the shifting social power structures of the new America.

Smith-Howard and Heintzelman (2005) have noted the significance of the clash between Blanche and Stanley over the loss of Belle Reve in Scene II; what the plantation represents to each of them is powerfully suggestive. Belle Reve:

> **is Blanche's lost, beautiful dream, rich with family heritage and pride; Stanley is interested only in the property's material or monetary real estate value. He is happy in the loud, harsh, and dirty world of the Vieux Carré of New Orleans, whereas Blanche prefers finer accommodations, the bucolic setting of hundreds of acres of land and large white pillars on a grand veranda that provide lounging quarters out of the midday sun.**

Ironically the Belle Reve Blanche lost was in fact a very twisted version of this 'lost beautiful dream'; a Gothic horror straight out of the nightmare stories of Poe.

Stanley is an immigrant industrial worker who lives in Elysian Fields (an appropriate setting for a war hero) but here Blanche's genteel values are totally out of context. Thus as emblems of the moribund Southern aristocracy on the one hand and an energetic immigrant community determined to make its way in the world on the other, Blanche and Stanley are engaged in a desperate struggle only one of them can win; Stanley declares just before he rapes her, 'We've had this date with each other from the beginning!' (p. 81). It is certainly possible to see Blanche as a lost soul trapped in limbo between the old world and the new; as Williams's great contemporary Elia Kazan put it, she is 'a last dying relic... now adrift in our unfriendly day'.

---

*Pause for **Thought*** ▮▮

The poet and critic T. S. Eliot coined the term 'objective correlative' to describe the way in which objects, situations or events are used to represent characters or emotions. How far do you think it is true to say that Belle Reve is the objective correlative for Blanche's identity as a Southern belle?

Taking it ▶
Further ▶

G. P. A. Healy's famous portrait *The Southern Belle* (1860) shows the beautiful Miss Sallie Ward of Louisville, Kentucky, in her prime. You can view the painting online at www.speedmuseum.org. Follow the route Collection — American Art — The Kentucky Collection — George Peter Alexander Healey.

❰ Top ten *quotation*

Gender roles

During the Second World War women had become used to filling the men's roles in the workplace and had gained considerable freedom and financial independence; for a while it had seemed possible for women to pursue their own version of the American Dream. *A Streetcar Named Desire* presents a sharp critique of the way the institutions and attitudes of postwar America affected women's lives, just as later, in *Cat on a Hot Tin Roof*, the rivalry between Maggie and Mae raises questions about the role of college-educated women in the 1950s and the extent to which they were still defined by their fertility and domesticity. Many of Williams's female characters seem psychologically trapped in the cultural pragmatics of the Old South, as Blanche and Stella's dependence on men exposes attitudes to women during the transition from the old world to the new. Both Blanche and Stella — and Eunice, for that matter — see male companions as their only means to achieve happiness and depend on men for both economic and psychological reasons. When Stanley uses the Napoleonic code to try to muscle in on Stella's inheritance it seems exploitative, yet Blanche's escape plan (throwing herself on the mercy of Shep Huntleigh) still involves playing a submissive and dependent role. Ironically, when Blanche invokes the vision of Shep arriving to rescue her in Scene XI, it is in fact the doctor who offers her his gentlemanlike support when he escorts her to the asylum.

Literary context

Intertextuality

The influential French feminist and literary theorist Julia Kristeva (b. 1941) coined the term 'intertextuality' in 1966 to describe the complex network of links which exist between texts. Working with Kristeva's notion of intertextuality allows us to place *Streetcar* at the centre of a web of interconnected texts and contexts that show just how fascinating and challenging the play remains, almost 70 years after it was written.

Southern Gothic

Feminist critic Molly Haskell, herself a Southerner, has described:

> ...the attraction of the Lost Cause mythology — we were grander, purer in defeat than were those crass, winner-

take-all Yankees with their greedy industrial culture.
The myth of the Lost Cause and the moral superiority of
losing defined and fed our romantic sense of ourselves, our
specialness, our region marked by a defeat that wasn't quite
a defeat in a war that wasn't quite over.   (M. Haskell,
          Frankly, My Dear: 'Gone with the Wind' Revisited, 2009)

As a writer closely associated with the Southern Gothic genre, Williams
overhauls and deconstructs the traditional stereotype of the demure
Southern belle by making Blanche DuBois not just the damsel in
distress she pretends to be for her naïve suitor Mitch's benefit, but also a
promiscuous alcoholic who threatens to trash her sister's marriage.

Williams once described Southern Gothic as allied with 'an underlying
dreadfulness in modern experience' and his adoption of the nickname
'Tennessee' was an acknowledgement of his conscious commitment
to dramatising the culture, values and conflicts of his native land. In
'Person-to-Person', Williams captured the tragicomic desperation of the
Southern experience in general and the Southern writer in particular in
this memorable vignette:

> I once saw a group of little girls on a Mississippi sidewalk,
> all dolled up in their mothers' and sisters' cast-off finery,
> old raggedy ball gowns and plumed hats and high-heeled
> slippers, enacting a meeting of ladies in a parlour with a
> perfect mimicry of Southern gush and simper. But one child
> was not satisfied with the attention paid her performance
> by the others...so she stretched out her skinny arms and
> threw back her skinny neck and shrieked to the deaf
> heavens and her equally oblivious playmates, 'Look at me,
> look at me, look at me!'
>
> And then her mother's high-heeled slippers threw her off
> balance and she fell to the sidewalk in a great howling
> tangle of soiled white satin and torn pink net, and still
> nobody looked at her.
>
> I wonder if she is not, now, a Southern writer.
>   (Williams, *Cat on a Hot Tin Roof*, 1976)

Williams's contemporary Flannery O'Connor, one little girl who did grow
up to be a Southern writer, noted with irony the cultural divide between
the North and the South:

> ...anything that comes out of the South is going to be called
> grotesque by the northern reader, unless it is grotesque, in
> which case it is going to be called realistic.

> Williams's...
> adoption of
> the nickname
> 'Tennessee' was an
> acknowledgement
> of his conscious
> commitment to
> dramatising the
> culture, values and
> conflicts of his
> native land

*Pause for **Thought***

It is interesting to compare Williams's dramatic representations of the South (and its women) with the work of some female prose writers associated with the Southern Gothic genre. You might begin by dipping into Carson McCullers' *The Ballad of the Sad Cafe* (1951), Harper Lee's *To Kill a Mockingbird* (1960), Flannery O'Connor's *Everything That Rises Must Converge* (1965) or Donna Tartt's *The Little Friend* (2002).

Like O'Connor and many other practitioners working within the Southern Gothic genre, Williams dramatises with both humour and pathos the apparent inability of the genteel gracious gallantry of the mythic antique Old South to survive amid the brash consumerist confidence of booming postwar America, and never more powerfully than in *Streetcar*, in which this debate is framed around the binary oppositions embodied by Stanley and Blanche, the future and the past.

Finally, when the doctor arrives at the end of *Streetcar* to escort Blanche to the lunatic asylum, he ironically conforms to the heroine's outdated notion of the chivalrous Southern beau who will offer her the gentlemanly support and kindness she craves so desperately. Her ultimate collapse can be seen as the apocalyptic meltdown of an entire semi-mythological culture.

The epigraph: Hart Crane

> And so it was I entered the broken world
> To trace the visionary company of love, its voice
> An instant in the wind [I know not whither hurled]
> But not for long to hold each desperate choice.

The epigraph to *A Streetcar Named Desire* is the fifth stanza of Hart Crane's poem 'The Broken Tower'. Williams admired and identified with Crane (1899–1932) and there are significant parallels between their lives; both had difficult relationships with their parents, struggled with alcoholism and were trying to find their identities as gay men at a time when there was still intense social and cultural stigma attached to homosexuality. Like the tortured young poet Allan Grey in *Streetcar*, Hart Crane committed suicide at a tragically young age; because 'The Broken Tower' was the last poem he wrote before his death, some readers have seen it as akin to his last will and testament. As Gilbert Debusscher has noted, '[a]mong the few permanent possessions Williams took with him on his constant peregrinations were a copy of Hart Crane's collected poems and a framed portrait of the poet' (Debusscher in Roudané, 1997). Williams made sure that the epigraph was printed in the theatre programmes to make it as easy for an audience to compare Crane's words with his drama as for a reader; the poem captures a sense of love as a transitory illusion or gambler's 'desperate choice', which is strongly suggestive of Blanche's experience of love in a 'broken world'.

*Pause for **Thought***

You can read the full text of 'The Broken Tower' online: go to **http://oldpoetry.com** and search on 'Harold Hart Crane'; click on 'The Broken Tower'.

Romanticism

Romanticism (c. 1770–1830) was a European cultural phenomenon which encompassed not only literature in all its forms but also art, music, politics, philosophy, science and religion. Set against a historical background of radical change in which traditional social, religious, economic and political beliefs were challenged and reinterpreted, it followed on from and partly rebelled against the previous age of Enlightenment, preferring originality, imagination and freedom to reason, self-restraint and order.

The word *Romantic* is linked to the French word *romance* and implies a search for meaning and identity. The Romantics believed that artists should seek the essential truth about life and mediate that truth through their own personal experiences. Their quintessential archetype was the Byronic hero, an anti-Establishment outcast who hovered on the margins of mainstream society, questioning its values, conventions and ideas. The origin of this archetype was the poet Lord Byron himself, a legendary figure whose significance as a cultural icon proved hugely influential both during his own lifetime and for generations to come. Above all, Byron's wandering exile has come to symbolise the Romantic quest for freedom, mobility and space in a harsh and unsympathetic world.

In many ways Williams himself was just such an artistic and cultural outsider, 'a poet in a practical world, a homosexual in a heterosexual society', as Nancy M. Tischler has written (Tischler in Roudané, 1997). Williams, like Byron, Poe and Crane, was a misfit whose imagination and poetic spirit left him out of tune with the pragmatic mores of his contemporary society. He regretted the loss of the South's traditional creed of elegance, beauty and gallantry and his plays are scattered with romantic dreamers like Blanche — and himself — tragically out of place in the new America and driven to use sex, alcohol and often drugs as a means of escape. The interweaving of his lush, sometimes grandiose romantic visions and the grimy reality of ordinary life is one of the hallmarks of Williams's life and work, and in *Streetcar* the clash between Romanticism and pragmatism is encapsulated by the opposing figures of Blanche and Stanley.

Context

The public image of George Gordon, Lord Byron (1788–1824) played as great a role in his success as did his poetry. Lionised by literary London, he was run out of town when rumours spread about his unorthodox love life; he had an affair with his half-sister and was sexually attracted to young boys. By 1816 he was living a nomadic life abroad, in permanent exile from England. He died in Greece at the age of 36.

Context

The director Elia Kazan, who worked with Williams often, said: 'everything in his life is in his plays, and everything in his plays is in his life'. Williams himself said: 'I can't expose a human weakness on the stage unless I know it through having it myself.'

Parallels with *Cat on a Hot Tin Roof*

Cat on a Hot Tin Roof (1955) also dramatises Williams's ideas of history, family, religion and community and minutely deconstructs traditional Southern stereotypes as Williams entwines the tragic stories

of a powerful man who wrongly thinks he has cheated death and his once famous and idolised son. Both Big Daddy Pollitt and his younger son Brick can be viewed through the dramatic prism of classical and Shakespearian tragedy, as both characters are highly gifted but also deeply flawed. Brick's weary lethargy is reminiscent of Hamlet's inability to act decisively and face up to a family crisis, and perhaps even more resonant is Williams's decision to have the fallen sporting idol hobble about with his broken foot in a cast, given that the name 'Oedipus', the most famous of all tragic heroes, may be translated literally as 'swollen foot'.

This book has already mentioned several comparisons and connections between *Streetcar* and *Cat on a Hot Tin Roof*, but there are others:

- Like Blanche, Maggie can be seen as the archetypal demure Southern belle pining for a chivalrous beau viewed through a distorted lens. While many of the minor characters in *Streetcar* provide evidence of the easy, bustling multicultural nature of working-class New Orleans, in *Cat on a Hot Tin Roof* the comfortable caricature of the happy slave or 'Uncle Tom' is undermined by Williams's symbolic use of the Pollitt's black servants, never seen but heard off stage at key dramatic moments. When Mae cries, 'Oh Big Daddy, the field hands are singing for you!' the servants' chosen spiritual is 'Pick a bale of cotton', a song about the hardships of slavery which reminds the audience that the Pollitt inheritance was founded on the forced labour of thousands of black agricultural workers.

- Both texts deal with families and inheritance; up for grabs in *Cat on a Hot Tin Roof* is Big Daddy's $10 million fortune, '28,000 acres of the richest land this side of the valley Nile', and the family vultures are circling even before he realises he's dying. In *Streetcar*, although Belle Reve was lost before the action of the play begins, Stanley hopes, like (Mae and Gooper in *Cat*) that legal documents will prove his claim.

- Both Blanche and Brick prefer to live in the past, before the suicide of the homosexual characters they loved and lost. They are haunted by guilt at having responded harshly to Allan and Skipper respectively. (Like Allan, Skipper never appears on stage.)

- Brick and Blanche both use alcohol to numb their emotional pain and retreat to the bathroom in times of stress.

- Both Big Daddy's and Blanche's birthday parties end disastrously.

- Both plays metaphorically link desire and death, in that while Blanche's streetcar is heading for Cemeteries, Doc Baugh points out that it's a toss-up as to whether Mae's sixth baby will arrive before Big

Daddy dies of cancer — 'the stork and the reaper are running neck-and-neck'.

- The plays end with the real or imagined birth of a baby: Stella and Stanley's son and a projected one 'sired by Brick, and out of Maggie the Cat!'

- Blanche and Brick clash violently with Stanley and Big Daddy; in each case romantic ruin is offset with brute strength and vigorous vulgarity.

- The cheap collapsible camp-bed upon which Stanley rapes Blanche is paralleled by the huge double bed which dominates Brick and Maggie's bedroom in *Cat on a Hot Tin Roof*. This is the marital bed in which the glamorous young couple no longer make love; as Big Mama says, pointing at the bed, 'When a marriage goes on the rocks, the rocks are *there*, right *there*!'

*Pause for **Thought*** ⏸

How far do you think *Cat on a Hot Tin Roof*'s great showdown between Brick and Big Daddy might be seen as wish-fulfilment: the dialogue Williams never had with his own harsh father, who despised him as a 'sissy'?

Performance context

The 1951 Kazan film

Vivien Leigh and Marlon Brando

Vivien Leigh was a Hollywood celebrity who had won an Academy Award for her iconic performance as the wilful and beautiful Southern belle Scarlett O'Hara in *Gone with the Wind* (1939). Adapted from

Vivien Leigh as Scarlett O'Hara on the family's plantation in the film *Gone with the Wind* (1939)

Selznick/MGM/The Kobal Collection

Margaret Mitchell's 1936 novel, *Gone with the Wind* is still probably the most famous film ever made and certainly the high-water mark of Hollywood's golden age. Leigh was a little-known English actress when she won the part of Scarlett in a blaze of publicity following a three-year search for the perfect heroine; if not quite the rags-to-riches cliché of the understudy who becomes an overnight star, it was as close as made no difference.

The beautiful, flirtatious and yet innocent belle was the quintessential pattern of ideal young womanhood among the aristocracy of the doomed Old South, and in *Gone With The Wind* Scarlett O'Hara's story plays out against the epic backdrop of the American Civil War. As Molly Haskell suggests, Scarlett is a fascinating character:

> **poised at one of those pivotal moments in the redefining**
> **of women's roles...when the entire catechism of traditional**
> **womanly virtues — piety, chastity, sacrifice, living through**
> **and for others, and unflagging loyalty to family and**
> **country — virtues held up since time immemorial, seem**
> **to be turned on their head! In their place are offered such**
> **alarmingly worldly aspirations as self-fulfilment, sexual**
> **freedom, mobility, choice, and appetite for things beyond**
> **home and family.** **(Haskell, 2009)**

It is worth bearing in mind that *Gone with the Wind*'s most famous location, Tara, the fabled plantation which Scarlett adores, would have been the iconic template evoked in the minds of most of Williams's contemporaries with every mention of Belle Reve in *A Streetcar Named Desire*. While Blanche is far more fragile than the feisty Scarlett, as John Russell Taylor has noted:

> **...she does set one wondering what happened to that kind**
> **of Southern belle with the passage of time and the decay**
> **of the South, and Scarlett's obsession with Tara is well**
> **matched by Blanche's with Belle Reve. More specifically,**
> **what would have become of Scarlett when she had aged and**
> **her beauty faded to a degree that she could not always get**
> **her own way just by stamping her little foot?**
> **(J. R. Taylor, *Vivien Leigh*, 1984)**

Legend has it that while Leigh was not director Elia Kazan's first choice to play Blanche in the 1951 film version of *A Streetcar Named Desire*, he was intrigued by the idea of watching Scarlett O'Hara go mad. Jessica Tandy, who played Blanche in the original Broadway stage production, was in any case not a big enough box-office star to headline an edgy production which dealt with rape, promiscuity and homosexuality. Given that Leigh's role as Scarlett meant that for a whole generation of cinema-goers she simply *was* the archetypal belle of American popular culture, her wrecked and ruined turn as Williams's belle gone bad seems to capture something of the apparently inevitable decline of the South itself.

Whereas Leigh was Hollywood royalty, the casting of Marlon Brando as Stanley offers a sense of life shadowing art. At first mocked by traditionalists for his 'mumbling' delivery, he was instantly acclaimed by the younger generation as a groundbreaking new acting talent; according to film director Martin Scorsese, he was 'the marker': 'There's "before Brando" and "after Brando."' Unlike the classically trained Leigh, Marlon Brando was closely associated with the modern 'Method' school of acting. Working with the ideas of the Russian actor and director Konstantin Stanislavski, 'Method' actors sought to tap into the psychology of their characters in order to inhabit them more fully.

In some ways the fundamental contrast between Brando and Leigh as practitioners of their craft echoes the unbridgeable gulf between Stanley and Blanche, yet to the surprise of many, in the words of the film critic Pauline Kael, this chalk-and-cheese combination gave 'two of the greatest performances ever put on film', with Leigh's Blanche 'one of those rare performances that can truly be said to evoke both fear and pity'. Leigh herself, who suffered from periodic bouts of manic depression and mental illness, admitted, 'I had nine months in the theatre of Blanche DuBois. Now she's in command of me.' Indeed, while Williams felt Leigh's Blanche was 'everything that I intended, and much that I had never dreamed of', the actress herself felt that playing the role had 'tipped me over into madness'.

Given that the roles with which Leigh is indelibly associated reflect the same mythic cultural archetype of the Southern belle, it seems fitting that at the 1951 Academy Awards she was named Best Actress for playing Blanche DuBois just as she had been for Scarlett O'Hara 12 years before. Karl Malden and Kim Hunter also won Oscars as Best Supporting Actor and Actress for their portrayals of Mitch and Stella, but the Academy failed to acknowledge Marlon Brando's electrifying portrayal of Stanley despite its having established him as perhaps the greatest film actor of the postwar era. Even in later years, when his fatal cocktail of hubristic arrogance and self-indulgence had virtually destroyed his career, his rare screen appearances were still greeted as major cultural events. Appropriately enough, his most famous screen performance was as another working-class outsider determined to find his own inverted version of the American Dream — Vito Corleone, the penniless Sicilian

immigrant who becomes a Mafia don in Francis Ford Coppola's *The Godfather* (1972).

Changes from stage to screen

Several of the changes from stage to screen made in the 1951 Kazan film suggest that what was acceptable to an elite, sophisticated, minority Broadway theatre audience was unacceptable in a mainstream, conservative Hollywood film production context. Bound as it was by the notoriously restrictive film Production Code, as R. Barton Palmer notes, Hollywood 'was committed to banishing from significant representation or often mere mention the themes Williams found so compelling and unavoidable'. In effect, the Code dictated that films had to 'be structured by the central principle of nineteenth-century melodrama: evil was to be punished and good rewarded, while any sympathy for wrongdoing should be eliminated by compensating moral value (such as the unlikely reform in the last five minutes of hitherto enthusiastic sinners)'.

Streetcar's exploration of many areas of human existence which the Code defined as off-limits — alcoholism, promiscuity, rape, homosexuality and madness — was problematic enough, while the fact that Stanley's rape of his sister-in-law goes officially unpunished created a particular dilemma, even if Blanche's own sexual transgressions meant that 'suffering for a less-than-virtuous female main character did not violate then-acceptable notions of a poetically just ending' (Barton Palmer in Roudané, 1997).

At this point, it is worth setting *Streetcar* against the highly specific cultural context of the signature movie genre of the 1940s, the *film noir* (from the French for 'black cinema'). The leading female characters of these sexy, cynical and stylish crime melodramas were often treacherous *femmes fatales* who broke the rules of mainstream society and were brutally punished for their actions, while their male counterparts were often cynical private detectives bent on ferreting out their guilty secrets; there are obvious ironic parallels here with the roles of Blanche and Stanley. As Barton Palmer has noted, since the *film noir* genre popular at the time frequently featured attractive but morally ambiguous *femmes fatales* who wound up 'dead, imprisoned, or otherwise punished', *Streetcar*'s shocking conclusion 'would be acceptable to filmgoers used to similar portrayals of feminine misadventure'.

After the film was completed, however, the censors demanded certain cuts and alterations which were made without the consent of either

Taking it **Further**

Watch a classic *film noir* such as *Laura* (1944), *Double Indemnity* (1945) or *The Postman Always Rings Twice* (1946) and compare the sexual tension that exists between the male and female leads with Williams's portrayal of Blanche and Stanley in *A Streetcar Named Desire*. You can find out more about the *noir* genre online at **www.filmnoirstudies. com**.

Williams or director Elia Kazan, as Smith-Howard and Heintzelman (2005) note.

The major cuts were:

- several close-up shots which overtly emphasised the sexual passion between Stanley and Stella.
- the rape scene, leaving Stanley's attack implied rather than obvious.
- several references to Blanche's promiscuous past.
- several of Stanley's most sexually suggestive remarks to Blanche, such as his comment just before the rape: 'Come to think of it — maybe you wouldn't be bad to — interfere with...' (p. 80).

The major alteration was to the ending of the play. The censors did not wish to have Stanley appear to 'get away with' his near-incestuous rape, so the famous final 'Holy Family' tableau of Stella, Stanley and the baby was removed. Instead, Stella rebels against Stanley, seizing the baby and telling him: 'We're never going back. Never, never back. Never back again.' The film closes with her running upstairs to Eunice, as she did at the end of the poker night, while once again Stanley bellows: 'STELL-LAHHHHHH!'

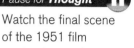

*Pause for **Thought***

Watch the final scene of the 1951 film version two or three times and compare it closely to the printed text. Given its very close parallels with the end of Scene III (the Poker Night), how likely is it, in your opinion, that Stella really will leave Stanley this time, as the film suggests?

Critical context

AO3 requires you to demonstrate an understanding that the meaning of a text is not 'fixed' and that at various places within a text different interpretations are possible. These different interpretations may be supported by reference to the ideas of named critics or particular critical perspectives, but may also emerge from your own discussions with other students and your teacher. As indicated in the section on 'Working with AO3', what matters is that you have come to a personal interpretation of the play through an understanding of a variety of ways of making meanings.

Critical approaches

Ways of thinking about texts

In 1968 the French literary theorist Roland Barthes wrote a hugely influential essay called *The Death of the Author* in which he argued that the idea of an author or authority led people to believe it was possible to

decode and hence explain the essential 'meaning' of a text. For Barthes, the multiple different ways of making meaning in language, and the fact that it is impossible to know the author's state of mind, made a mockery of the idea of a 'knowable text'. The Marxist Barthes saw the concept of the author as another method of transforming a text into a consumer product which could be used up and replaced in a bourgeois, westernised capitalist culture.

While the 'death of the author' theory might at first seem to suggest that Barthes effectively cut the reader's safety rope and left him or her dangling off a literary cliff, in fact his ideas can be seen as heralding the 'birth of the reader'. The reader-response approach to literature suggests that writers and readers collaborate to make meanings and that as readers our responses will depend upon our own experiences, ideas and values. Unlike literary theories or critical positions which concentrate on the author, content or form of the text, reader-response theory privileges the role of the active reader in creating textual meanings. If you remember this, you may well feel more confident in assessing the performances, interpretations and literary-critical points of view you encounter. Moreover by setting the play at the centre of an intertextual web of contexts and connections you can start to trace the assumptions underlying both *Streetcar* itself and the responses of various readers and audiences to the text. By resisting the notion of fixed meanings, you are free to make the most of the shifting and unstable nature of the text itself and do well in AO3 and AO4 assessment into the bargain. Thus while this section covers a variety of modern critical approaches that can shed considerable light on the play, remember that you too are a critic, and as such you should always try to form your own interpretation of the text.

Taking it ▶
Further

As well as Roland Barthes, other critics closely associated with reader-response include the German Wolfgang Iser (1926–2007) and the American Stanley Fish (b. 1938). You might wish to research their ideas using the internet and see how far you think they might be applied to *Streetcar* and the other texts you are studying for A-level.

Feminist criticism

Feminist criticism challenges assumptions about gender and exposes both the sexual stereotyping embodied in a text and the way in which such stereotypes might be subverted. Feminist critics attempt to describe and interpret women's experience as depicted in literature. They question long-standing dominant patriarchal attitudes, ideologies and interpretations and challenge traditional ideas about how women are (according to male writers) supposed to feel, act and think. Whether *Streetcar* exhibits feminist sympathies or merely accepts the patriarchal status quo, sexual double standard and cultural misogyny of its time is an issue that can only enhance your analysis of the roles of Blanche, Stella and even Eunice.

As Felicia Hardison Londré suggests, Scene IV 'strongly invites feminist criticism', since Blanche's only solution to what she sees as Stella's degraded life with Stanley is to look up her old beau Shep Huntleigh. While she sees Stanley as a brutal ape, as Londré points out:

> ...there is a subtle irony in her reflexive reversion to the Southern belle's habits of thought — that is, emotional dependence on a patriarchal system of male protection for the helpless female — just moments after she has said, 'I'm going to do something. Get hold of myself and make myself a new life!'
>
> (Londré in Roudané, 1997)

Political criticism

Political criticism might include Marxist analysis and New Historicism. It reminds us that literary texts are products of a particular set of socio-political circumstances from which they cannot be divorced, and that they are informed by a range of cultural preoccupations and anxieties that manifest themselves regardless of whether they are consciously intended by the writer or not. Marxist critics see literary texts as material products which are part of — and help to explain — the processes of history, as Terry Eagleton notes:

> Marxist criticism is not merely a 'sociology of literature', concerned with how novels get published and whether they mention the working class. Its aim is to explain the literary work more fully; and this means a sensitive attention to its forms, styles and meanings. But it also means grasping those forms, styles and meanings as the product of a particular history.
>
> (T. Eagleton, *Marxism and Literary Criticism*, 1976)

It was Williams's great contemporary Arthur Miller (1915–2005) who recognised that, although not an overtly 'political' playwright like Miller himself, Williams was still very much engaged with the warp and weft of contemporary American society. For Miller, a character like Blanche DuBois, whose waning social, political and economic authority encapsulates the uneasy tension between the legendary romantic ante-bellum South and its terrible history of slavery and oppression, is by definition clearly and heavily politicised.

According to Christopher Bigsby, however, Williams (who only voted once in his life) was if anything a 'profoundly conservative' writer. 'What he wanted above all was for the individual to be left alone, insulated

---

Pause for *Thought*

In your opinion is Blanche's 'emotional dependence' just part of the play's social context, or is it specific to her character?

Do you think Stella any less 'emotionally dependent' than her sister?

Context

The German philosopher and political thinker Karl Marx (1818–83) was the founder of modern communism. In *The Communist Manifesto* (1848), Marx stated: 'The history of all hitherto existing society is the history of class struggles.' Thus a Marxist literary critical perspective sees works of literature as inevitably conditioned by and reflective of the economic and political forces of their social context.

Pause for **Thought**

Arguably the fact that Stanley and Blanche clash so ferociously over economic issues reveals the increasingly consumerist and materialistic nature of the American Dream, and a Marxist reading of *Streetcar* might suggest that human relationships are inevitably warped and distorted by the forces of a capitalist social and political system. How far do you agree with this view?

Taking it **Further**

Read the full text of Miller's hugely influential short essay online at http://theliterarylink.com/miller1.html.

from the pressure of public event', although 'even if his radicalism is better viewed as a celebration of the outcast or the deprived, a sympathy for those discarded by a society for which he anyway had little sympathy, his work reveals a consistent distrust of the wealthy and powerful, a suspicion of materialism' (Bigsby, *Modern American Drama*, 2000).

In his 1949 essay 'Tragedy and the Common Man', Miller tried to define what it was that still moved contemporary audiences when watching a classical tragedy, given that the contexts of production and reception were so far removed from each other, and that therefore we cannot care very much about 'the right of one monarch to capture the domain from another' when 'our concepts of justice [are not] what they were to the mind of an Elizabethan king'. Instead, Miller argued:

> **The quality in such plays that does shake us, however, derives from the underlying fear of being displaced, the disaster inherent in being torn away from our chosen image of what or who we are in this world. Among us today this fear is as strong, and perhaps stronger, than it ever was. In fact, it is the common man who knows this fear best.**

Furthermore, he added:

> **...if it is true to say that in essence the tragic hero is intent upon claiming his whole due as a personality, and if this struggle must be total and without reservation, then it automatically demonstrates the indestructible will of man to achieve his humanity. The possibility of victory must be there in tragedy. Where pathos rules, where pathos is finally derived, a character has fought a battle he could not possibly have won. The pathetic is achieved when the protagonist is...incapable of grappling with a much superior force...But tragedy requires a nicer balance between what is possible and what is impossible. And it is curious, although edifying, that the plays we revere, century after century, are the tragedies. In them, and in them alone, lies the belief — optimistic, if you will, in the perfectibility of man. It is time, I think, that we who are without kings, took up this bright thread of our history and followed it to the only place it can possibly lead in our time — the heart and spirit of the average man.**

One very interesting outcome of trying to apply Miller's ideas to *Streetcar* is the extent to which it seems easier to fit Stanley into his 'common man' tragic paradigm than Blanche. It certainly appears true to say that both characters might be seen as sharing 'the underlying fear of being displaced, the disaster inherent in being torn away from our chosen image of what or who we are in this world' and thus 'intent upon claiming [their] whole due as a personality'. Yet beyond this, surely Blanche's struggle would be defined as pathetic rather than tragic in Miller's eyes, since she is so clearly fighting 'a battle [s]he could not possibly have won' and is 'incapable of grappling with a much superior force'. Stanley's battle, on the other hand, is 'total and without reservation' and thus 'automatically demonstrates the indestructible will of man to achieve his humanity'. Once again, it seems, the vexed debate about the identity of the hero and anti-hero — the protagonist and the antagonist — of *Streetcar* can be thrown wide open.

Psychoanalytic criticism

Sigmund Freud published one of the founding texts of psychoanalysis, *The Interpretation of Dreams*, in 1900. Psychoanalytic critics see literature as like dreams. Both are fictions, inventions of the mind that, although based on reality, are not literally true. Psychoanalytic criticism explores the significance of the subconscious as a means of exploring the representation of character. Much psychoanalytical criticism is based on the theories of Freud, and explores the effect of dreams, fantasies, unconscious desires and aspects of sexuality. In *A Streetcar Named Desire*, aspects of the text that lend themselves to psychoanalytic readings include Blanche's flashbacks and nightmares, the linking of sex and death and the overtly sexual nature of much of the imagery of the play.

In Freudian terms, two sexual traumas — one in the past (her discovery of Allan's homosexuality) and one in the present (her rape) — destroy Blanche's fragile hold on sanity. She attempts to repress her memories of the past through taking refuge in art, music and literature — as well as lots of illicit and unauthorised sex. For most modern readers, it is hard not to read the streetcar which 'bangs through the Quarter, up one old narrow street and down another' (p. 40) as a graphically blunt metaphor for the sexual act itself, while the phallic symbolism of the poker game (in which 'one-eyed jacks are wild' and the game is 'seven-card stud', pp. 24–25) seems equally ominous. Moreover the polarised streetcar destinations of Desire and Cemeteries certainly lend themselves to being considered in terms of Freud's belief that humans are motivated by two conflicting central desires, *eros* (which is creative, life-producing and

*Pause for **Thought***

Blanche hands the documents over to Stanley, saying: 'I think it's wonderfully fitting that Belle Reve should finally be this bunch of old papers in your big, capable hands!' (p. 22). Later she tells Stella 'maybe he's what we need to mix with our blood now that we've lost Belle Reve' (p. 23). Robert Bray interprets this as a transfer of power from the rural Old South to the industrial new America (Londré in Roudané, 1997). What do you think?

❮ Top ten *quotation*

thus drives sexual passion and love) and its opposite, *thanatos*, the death instinct, which wills us towards calm, oblivion and death.

Queer theory

The term 'queer theory' was only coined in 1990, but since the late 1960s, as Martin Ryan notes, 'gay and lesbian scholars who had up till then remained silent regarding their sexuality *or* the presence of homosexual themes in literature began to speak' (M. Ryan, *Literary Theory*, 1999). Queer theory is grounded in a debate about whether a person's sexuality is part of their essential self or socially constructed, and queer theorists question the ways in which heterosexuality is presented as 'normal' and focus on 'non-heteronormative' sexual behaviour. Queer theory is a particularly interesting way of looking at the life and work of Williams because, as Sean McEvoy has noted:

> **Many of Williams's characters are female. Some critics have claimed that these characters are projections of gay personal and social crises and that Williams was forced to represent these tragic issues through female characters because of the period's public intolerance of homosexuality.**
> **(McEvoy, 2009)**

As Christopher Bigsby suggests, Williams's outsider status may be seen as one of the reasons he became a master of the dramatic form, a genre which, by definition, involves multiple ways of making meaning:

> **Since Williams is the poet of the unauthorised, the unsanctioned, the outlawed, it seems logical that he should choose a form which more easily releases its pluralism of meanings — under the pressure of actors, director, audience — than does the poem or the novel. It is not that novels have restrictive meanings but that the incompletions of the theatrical text are readily apparent, indeed implicit in the form.**
> **(Bigsby, 2000)**

Moreover, as Miller argued in his autobiography *Timebends* (1987), Williams's identity as a gay man inevitably politicised both his life and his art:

> **If only because he came up at a time when homosexuality was absolutely unacknowledged in a public figure, Williams had to belong to a minority culture and understood in his bones what a brutal menace the majority could be if aroused against him…Certainly I never regarded him as the**

sealed-off aesthete he was thought to be. There is a radical politics of the soul as well as of the ballot box and the picket line. If he was not an activist it was not for the lack of a desire for justice, nor did he consider a theatre profoundly involved in society and politics...beyond his interest.

Performance criticism

Performance criticism looks at how the form of dramatic texts is determined by their basis in theatrical practice, examining them against what is known of the original stage conditions for which they were produced and the way they have been represented subsequently in other theatres and performance media. The approach looks at the essential elements of drama such as words, movement, sound, costume, setting and staging and questions the notion of a definitive version of a dramatic text, given that theatre is an essentially collaborative and ephemeral medium.

Streetcar has always been seen as one of Williams's masterworks, if not the best thing he ever did. As Felicia Hardison Londré has noted, there is no doubt about 'the centrality of *A Streetcar Named Desire* in his dramatic canon as well as in the American cultural consciousness'. She continues:

> Whether or not *A Streetcar Named Desire* is Tennessee Williams' 'best' play, or even his most performed play, it is probably the one most closely associated with the dramatist, and it is certainly the one that has elicited the most critical commentary. (Londré in Roudané, 1997)

In his own lifetime, among the major stars closely associated with Williams's work on stage and screen were Academy Award-winning Hollywood greats such as Marlon Brando, Vivien Leigh, Katharine Hepburn, Paul Newman and Elizabeth Taylor; their eagerness to work with him strongly suggests that his plays were seen to offer immense challenges and possibilities in performance terms. Arguably the symbiosis between Williams and these major actors suggests he had a significant impact on American cinema as well as upon the American stage. Moreover even three decades after his death it seems his plays can still sprinkle their stardust across a new generation of actors. In 2009, a new London stage production of *Streetcar* opened at the Donmar Warehouse and received admiring reviews. Rachel Weisz's Blanche was described by the critic Henry Hitchings in the *Evening Standard* as:

Taking it Further ➤

Critics closely associated with queer theory include the American critics Eve Kosofsky Sedgwick (1950–2009) and Adrienne Rich (b. 1929). You might wish to research their ideas using the internet and see how far you think they might be applied to *Streetcar* and the other texts you are studying for A-level.

Taking it Further ➤

Look at the rest of Henry Hitchings's review of the 2009 London stage production using the link below and see how far his response taps into your own ideas about the play. **www.thisislondon.co.uk** and search on 'Rachel Weisz mesmerizes'.

Taking it Further

In 1995 the composer and conductor André Previn wrote an opera based on *Streetcar* for which Philip Littell provided the lyrics. In his 2004 article 'The Media are Stepping on Our Toes' Jacques Coulardeau compares the original play with the 1951 film and the Previn/Littell opera and discusses the distinctive features of each genre. You can download a pdf of this article at: www.cercles. com/n10/coulardeau.pdf

Cleopatra by way of Miss Havisham, deliberately constructing a succession of roles (or disguises) for herself in order to keep reality at bay in a play which dramatises the tension between dark male impulses and feminine poise...[and] shows as well how vulgarity can bludgeon finer feelings into submission. Above all, it limns the destructiveness of desire. Blanche arrives on a streetcar at the cramped apartment in Elysian Fields that her sister Stella shares with Stanley. The vehicle's name, Desire, appears a symptom of the city's viscous sensuality, and the 'collapsible' bed in which she is expected to sleep symbolises the intriguingly uncertain social and sexual boundaries of her world — which are soon aggressively policed by Stanley.

Rachel Weisz received the Laurence Olivier Award for Best Actress for her performance, with Ruth Wilson being named Best Supporting Actress for her role as Stella. It seems the playwright Peter Shaffer was right when he commented:

He was a born dramatist as few are ever born. Whatever he put on paper, superb or superfluous, glorious or gaudy, could not fail to be electrifyingly actable. He could not write a dull scene...Tennessee Williams will live as long as drama itself.

Working with the text

Meeting the Assessment Objectives

Working with AO1

AO1: Articulate creative, informed and relevant responses to literary texts, using appropriate terminology and concepts, and coherent, accurate written expression.

To do well with AO1 you need to write fluently, structuring your essay carefully, guiding your reader clearly through your line of argument and using the sophisticated vocabulary, including critical terminology, which is appropriate to an A-level essay. You will need to use frequent embedded quotations to give evidence of close detailed knowledge, and you should demonstrate familiarity with the whole text. The ideal is to produce a well written academic essay employing appropriate discourse markers to create the sense of a shaped argument; it should use sophisticated terminology at times while remaining clear and cohesive.

Working with AO2

AO2: Demonstrate detailed critical understanding in analysing the ways in which form, structure and language shape meaning in literary texts.

Good students do not work only on a lexical level, but will also write well on the form and structure of the play, so in studying *Streetcar* it might be useful to begin with the larger elements of form and structure before considering language. If 'form is meaning', what are the implications of categorising the play as an American tragedy as opposed to a melodrama? The play is structured in a very distinctive way, as

further explored in the 'Form, structure and language' section of this book, and there has been much debate about the dramatic effectiveness of having 11 scenes as opposed to two or three acts. Then again, in order to discuss language in detail you will need to quote from the text — but the mere act of quoting is not enough to meet AO2. What is important is what you do with the quotation: how you analyse it and how it illuminates your argument. Moreover since you will at times need to make points about larger generic and organisational features of the play which are much too long to quote, being able to reference effectively is just as important as mastering the art of the embedded quotation. You could practise writing in analytical sentences, comprising a brief quotation or close reference, a definition or description of the feature you intend to analyse, an explanation of how this feature has been used and an evaluation of its effectiveness.

Working with AO3

AO3: Explore connections and comparisons between different literary texts and explore various interpretations, using these to develop your own.

AO3 is a double assessment objective which asks you to 'explore connections and comparisons' between texts as well as showing your understanding of the views and interpretations of others. If your examination board requires you to compare and contrast one or more other texts with *A Streetcar Named Desire* you must try to find specific points of comparison, rather than merely generalising.

You will find it easier to make comparisons and connections between texts (of any kind) if you try to balance them as you write; remember also that connections and comparisons are not only about finding similarities — differences are just as interesting. Above all, consider how the comparison illuminates each text. It is not just a matter of finding the relationships and connections but of analysing what they show. Some connections will be thematic, others generic or stylistic.

There are many ways in which *Streetcar* can be compared to other twentieth-century American stage classics such as Miller's *A View From the Bridge* (1955) or Edward Albee's *Who's Afraid of Virginia Woolf?* (1962) in terms of form, structure, language and theme. If you wish to explore thematic contrasts across different literary genres, you might, for example, trace a common theme such as love, the American Dream, the role of women, minds under stress, or appearance and reality. Overall, to do well with the first half of AO3 you must write about several worthwhile issues around narrative, genre, critical debate and context within a selective and balanced interweaving of your chosen texts.

To access the second half of AO3 effectively you need to measure your own interpretation of a text against those of other readers. By all means refer to named critics and quote from them if it seems appropriate, but the examiners are most interested in your personal and creative response. The best candidates produce fresh personal responses rather than merely regurgitating the ideas of others, be they teachers, fellow students or published academic authors, however famous or insightful these interpretations may be. However, as a text that has generated widely differing responses, *Streetcar* lends itself readily to the range of interpretations which have been noted in the 'Critical contexts' section of this book (pp. 63–70 of this guide).

Try to show an awareness of multiple readings with regard to the play as well as an understanding that (as Barthes suggested) its meaning is dependent as much upon what the reader brings to it as what Williams left there. Using modal verb phrases such as 'may be seen as', 'might be interpreted as' or 'could be represented as' implies that you are aware that different readers interpret texts in different ways at different times. The key word here is plurality; there is no single meaning, no right answer, and you need to evaluate a range of other ways of making textual meanings as you work towards your own. By all means refer to named critics and engage with their views to push forward your own argument, but above all try to convey an ambitious and conceptualised awareness of the fact that meanings in texts are shifting and unstable as opposed to fixed and immutable.

Working with AO4

AO4: Demonstrate understanding of the significance and influence of the contexts in which literary texts are written and received.

To access AO4 effectively means choosing your contexts carefully, showing detailed knowledge and understanding of how the contexts of production, reception, culture, society, history and genre can affect the ways in which we read *Streetcar* and assessing their impact with care. AO4, with its emphasis on the 'significance and influence' of the 'contexts in which literary texts are written and received', might at first seem less deeply rooted in the text itself, but in fact you are considering and evaluating here the relationship between the text and its contexts. Note the word 'received': this refers to the way interpretation can be influenced by the specific contexts within which the reader is operating.

When you are studying a text written some years ago, there is often a significant gulf between its original contemporary context of production and the twenty-first century context in which you receive it.

To access AO4 successfully you need to think about how contexts of production, reception, literature, culture, biography, geography, society, history, genre and intertextuality can affect texts. Place the play at the heart of the web of contextual factors which you feel have had the most impact upon it; examiners want to see a sense of contextual alertness woven seamlessly into the fabric of your essay rather than a clumsy bolted-on website rehash or some recycled history notes. Try to convey your awareness of the fact that literary works contain embedded and encoded representations of the cultural, moral, religious, racial and political values of the society from which they emerged, and that over time attitudes and ideas change until the views they reflect are no longer widely shared. And you're right to think that there must be an overlap between a focus on interpretations (AO3) and a focus on contexts, so do not worry about pigeonholing the AOs here.

Summary

Overall, the hallmarks of a successful A-level essay which demonstrates an engaged response to all four AOs should include:

- a clear introduction which orientates the reader and outlines your main proposal, debate or argument.
- a coherent, consistent and conceptualised argument which relates to the question title.
- confident movement around the text to support the argument rather than a relentless chronological trawl through it.
- apt and effective quotations or textual references embedded and adapted to make sense within the context of your own sentence.
- a wide range of effective points about the form, structure and language of the text.
- a strong and personally engaged awareness of how a text can be interpreted by different readers and audiences in different ways at different times.
- a sense that you are prepared to take on a good range of critical and theoretical perspectives.
- a conclusion which effectively summarises and consolidates your response and relates it back to your essay title.

Writing assignments

The first and most important thing to remember is that the text itself will lie at the heart of your study, whether you are studying the play for coursework or for examination. Therefore, although you may need to become familiar with such elements of the course as the format and style of examination questions and the four Assessment Objectives, nothing will be as significant as your own close knowledge of the text.

The second important thing to remember is the crucial issue of relevance. Whether you are writing in response to an examination question you have never seen before or a coursework task that you have discussed in detail with your teacher you will get no credit for including material that is off-task or tangential.

Finally, expect to have to approach the text in different ways, depending on the form of your examination response. Traditional coursework and controlled conditions assessment; open and closed book examinations; conventional literary analysis and re-creative or transformational writing; studied or unseen texts all require distinctively different approaches which you will have to prepare for carefully with your teacher.

The suggested approaches, tasks and titles that follow can be used to help you get to grips with *A Streetcar Named Desire* in a number of ways. They can be used as a stimulus for class discussions, presentations, collaborative work or peer assessment activities, for individual revision, timed or extended writing practice, or to provide ideas for potential coursework titles. However you use them, though, you will need to refer closely to the text to support your arguments and comments with succinct and relevant evidence. Try, too, to demonstrate an awareness of the ideas of other readers by incorporating relevant critical material, where appropriate, as a basis for the development of your own personal argument and response.

Examples of possible essay titles and selected student responses to them are given here; there are more in the Downloads section of the free website which accompanies this book, at **www.philipallan.co.uk/ literatureguidesonline.**

Traditional coursework tasks

Wider reading is very important at A-level and you may need to compare and contrast *Streetcar* with another text or texts you have studied.

Sometimes this text will be set for you by your exam board or chosen by your teacher, and sometimes the choice of comparative text(s) will be up to you. Clearly you will need to compare and contrast your chosen texts effectively, but beyond this you need to check the appropriate weightings for the relevant AOs as laid down by your particular exam board. AO1 will almost certainly be assessed throughout your essay, but you should plan carefully to ensure that you spend a proportionate amount of time and effort addressing the specific weightings and requirements of the other AOs.

As well as ensuring your title clearly addresses the relevant Assessment Objectives and allows for adequate, focused treatment within the set word limit, there are a number of crucial stages in the coursework writing process:

- Discuss your proposed title with your teacher as soon as possible.
- Set aside an hour to jot down ideas for the essay and convert them into an essay plan. Share this plan with your teacher and make use of any feedback offered.
- Identify any background reading, such as textual criticism, that may be useful to you, gather the books you need, read them and make notes.
- Give yourself a reasonable period to draft the essay, working with your text, your notes and other useful materials around you.
- Keep referring back to the title or question to make sure you remain focused on it.
- Allow time for your teacher to read and comment on your draft.
- Redraft and proofread your essay before handing it in and ensure that you have maintained your focus on the relevant AOs.
- A bibliography will add to the professionalism of your essay. This should list all the texts you have consulted. Check with your teacher whether you are required to use any particular format for a bibliography and stick to this.

Sample task

How far do you agree with the argument that Tennessee Williams's presentation of Blanche DuBois in *A Streetcar Named Desire* is less realistic than that of Maggie Pollitt in *Cat on a Hot Tin Roof*?

Transformational writing

Another type of coursework task is the popular transformative option in which you must show your awareness of genre, context and the intricacies of language through a piece of creative writing. This kind of hands-on approach is certainly not an easier option than the traditional literary criticism essay, as it requires you to unify creative and critical textual approaches; you must analyse Williams's choices of form, structure and language in detail before attempting to intervene in the text itself. Working with your source text, you may have to create a new scene or speech, retell part of the story from an alternative viewpoint or change the genre altogether, which will mean reading and re-reading the play actively and imaginatively. Your aim should be to produce an original written response which remains rooted convincingly within the original play.

Sample task

Write a conversation between Stella and Eunice which takes place when they are helping to pack Blanche's trunk before she leaves Elysian Fields for the asylum. You should aim to build upon Tennessee Williams's presentation of their characters and capture aspects of his chosen form, structure and language. You should also produce a brief commentary which analyses the particular effects you have tried to create and how these relate back to the original source text.

Sample answer

EUNICE is half-heartedly trying to pack BLANCHE's trunk as STELLA stares into space, rhythmically rocking the baby's cradle. Suddenly, EUNICE is still for a moment, before retracing the palm of her hand carefully across the tattered satin lining. With surprisingly delicacy she slips her fingers inside and extracts an old sepia photograph which has obviously been hiding there for the longest time. Squinting at it, EUNICE looks over at the unseeing Madonna beside her, apparently seeking and finding a resemblance.

EUNICE: My stars, Stella Kowalski! Look at this here old picture. Can this be you and Blanche? It's got something scrawled on the back of it, but the pencil's nearly worn right off so you can't hardly read it.

EUNICE shows STELLA a dog-eared, well-thumbed, much-mended picture of the two sisters on the steps of Belle Reve in a better and gentler time. Blanche is a beautiful sixteen in pale lace, Stella an awkward nine in schoolroom gingham. Blanche has a protective arm around Stella's

shoulders. *Both are smiling in blissful ignorance of what the morrow will bring.*

STELLA: *(stirring, recognising, marvelling)* Let me see that old thing. Why, would you look at that! I haven't seen that picture in a lifetime!

EUNICE: *(scrutinising the photograph intently and holding it up to the light, teasingly)* My, my, Miz Stella DuBois, but ain't you a picture with them twin braids right down to your waist!

STELLA: Why, those braids were the absolute bane of my life! With all those terrible knots and tangles, I used to cry like a baby every time my Mama pulled and yanked at me with that mean old paddle brush. So rough, she was, I could hardly bear it. I'd howl and scream till she'd say, 'Lord alive, Miz Stella for star, I swear I'll shave your head if you don't quit fussing and behave like a little lady!' But then, just when me and Mama were about fit to come to blows, Blanche would take pity on me, and ask Mama if she could be the one to brush out my hair before she went off dancing or to one of her parties in the evenings. A hundred strokes with a hairbrush before I said my prayers, she told me, that's what I should do every single night without fail. A real lady had to suffer to be beautiful, she said. But you know, Eunice, I never did suffer when Blanche did my hair — she was so gentle with me that I never felt a thing. And then she'd let me scramble into her bed and watch her put on one of her pretty dresses — like — *(She gestures towards Blanche's trunk in horror, staring at it as it gapes like an open wound, a violated thing in the centre of the room.)*

EUNICE: *(anxious to distract Stella)* She sure looks like a princess in this picture, right enough. How old was she then?

STELLA: Why, Blanche would be just sixteen when that picture was taken. That would be — let me think — oh yes! The late fall of 1930. That was the very night she met Allan Grey.

EUNICE: Who was that, honey? Her first beau?

STELLA: Goodness, no — he was her husband. My sister was a true child bride. And, my Lord, you must have guessed it, I was her flower girl. Oh my, but I was such a comical little thing — so plump and round and dumpy! But Blanche — why, she looked just beautiful and Allan was about the most handsome man I ever saw — like a prince right out of a fairy tale! *(She breaks off, clearly caught up in the memory of that day. Slowly and gently, with a melancholy and plangent tone, the Varsouviana begins to play.)* Even though I was sent right up to bed directly after the wedding speeches, I was much too giddy for sleep. So I sat myself right down as quiet as a little mouse on the upstairs landing at Belle Reve, and I peeped through the balustrade and watched Blanche and Allan dance their first dance as a married couple — the Varsouviana. I tell you, Eunice, I'd never seen such a romantic sight before, and I don't suppose I ever will again. It's just incredible to look back on that night now and to think that Allan's dead and Blanche — oh my God — Blanche! (*STELLA breaks off, and looks wildly about her, as if searching for her sister. The Varsouviana breaks off catastrophically, in a sudden, screaming fury.*)

EUNICE: (*gently, concerned*) He's dead? Oh my Lord. Poor Blanche. Was he killed in the war?

STELLA: (*fervently*) My God, I wish he had been! It would have been easier! Then there would have been a story that could have been told, instead of one so ugly and so dreadful that we all had to run and hide from it!

Student commentary

I decided to write my transformational piece using a blend of stage directions and dialogue because this is one of the fundamental aspects of Tennessee Williams's dramatic style. I also wanted to incorporate his signature technique of the non-naturalistic Varsouviana, but of course in *Streetcar* only Blanche ever hears this; thus I had to find a plausible reason for using it in a new context. I wanted to suggest that Stella is as haunted by guilt at rejecting her sister and condemning her to a living death in the asylum as Blanche was at helping to drive Allan Grey to suicide, thus tapping into Tennessee Williams's memory play genre. My solution was to add dramatic irony by making the Varsouviana not only the music Blanche and Allan were dancing to the night he died, but that it was also the theme they first danced to as man and wife at their wedding reception, which is why Stella associates it with them.

In terms of dialogue I have tried to make Stella's idiolect more refined and educated than Eunice's more colloquial and demotic working-class speech to suggest that talking about her life at Belle Reve transposes Stella into a very different context which unconsciously affects her language. Usually when Stella is on stage with Blanche or Stanley she has less dialogue, but here I wanted to make her memories the dramatic focus, so she has more to say than Eunice. Stella has longer, syntactically complex sentences whereas Eunice's are shorter and simpler to add variety, but also because often she is asking questions or prompting Stella to continue with her story. I reframed Stella's disgusted response to Allan Grey's homosexuality within the play —

she tells Stanley he was a 'degenerate' — to account for her strong outburst here, where she declares it would have been better for him to have been killed 'honourably' in battle.

In terms of context I tried not to be too obvious, but included references to the social and cultural divisions between rich and poor and I also felt that the postwar context would have led Eunice to assume that a young man who had died suddenly would have been killed in action. Beyond this I tried to reflect the Southern belle rules which would have been enforced on the DuBois sisters while they were growing up, and I made Stella chafe against these apparently silly restrictions because she did in the end rebel against her upbringing and escape to New Orleans, leaving Blanche to stick it out alone at Belle Reve.

Examiner's comments

AO1 — quality of writing:

- vocabulary wide, apt and appropriate for each character, showing their different social backgrounds, with many convincing echoes of Southern dialect
- creative, original and wholly convincing depiction of Stella's memories of Belle Reve
- accurately laid out according to dramatic conventions
- exceptionally well written with immaculate spelling, punctuation and grammar
- apt and informative commentary showing exemplary knowledge and understanding of the source text

AO2 — form, structure and language:

- clear use of the source text as a template with highly effective reflections of several key aspects of Williams's typical form, structure and language such as the memory play genre, verbal, visual and aural symbolism, the Varsouviana music, heightened dialogue and detailed stage directions
- clear sense of the whole text (e.g. tense and tragic atmosphere foreshadowing Blanche's eventual fate)
- specific reflections of the source text which show a seamless overarching understanding of text (e.g. relationship between Stella and Eunice and Stella and Blanche)
- sense that each character's language is 'a map of her mind'

AO3 — comparison and interpretations:

(The first part of AO3 — comparison — is not assessed in this task.)

- offers a fresh, subtle and convincing interpretation of Stella's motivation, thoughts, ideas and attitudes
- highly convincing sense that the characters have been understood and their language, ideas and relationship are consistent and likely, based on a close reading of the text

AO4 — context:

- subtle but clear references, actions and language appropriate to the era in which the text is set and in line with typical attitudes (e.g. Southern belle context; mentions of Belle Reve's grandeur; Blanche's willingness to 'suffer to be beautiful')

Overall:

This student has produced an excellent piece of work which fulfils all the criteria for a high Grade A.

'Critical debate' tasks

Examination questions often invite you to think about a possible view of the text and, by implication, go on to debate this. Any frame of words such as 'how far' or 'to what extent' implies that a straight 'yes or no' answer will not be enough and that you must construct a coherent argument.

Sample task

> **How far do you agree with the view that Stanley Kowalski should be seen as a Machiavellian villain rather than a working-class hero in Tennessee Williams's play *A Streetcar Named Desire*?**

Sample answer

When discussing Williams's presentation of Stanley Kowalski in *A Streetcar Named Desire* it is vital to set the play in its social, cultural and historical context by acknowledging that the character is used to epitomise the changing face of the new America after the Second World War. He is a super-confident alpha-male character whose behaviour towards women — his wife Stella and sister-in-law Blanche — allows Williams to debate big political themes through stock characters liable to be recognised by a contemporary audience.

Top ten **quotation** ⟩
Stanley bitterly resents Blanche's unthinkingly degrading comments, declaring: 'I am not a Polack. People from Poland are Poles, not Polacks. But what I am is a one hundred percent American, born and raised in the greatest country on earth and proud as hell of it, so don't ever call me a Polack.' A second-generation Polish American immigrant, his understandable patriotic pride in having served his country during the war makes him eager to gain the American Dream amid the cosmopolitan and socially flexible city of New Orleans and his positive 'can-do' attitude may well have been especially attractive to Williams's contemporary audience.

Similarly, although Stanley seems to dominate his wife Stella economically (she does not work outside the home), physically (he is violent to her) and sexually (the very first time we see him, he throws a package of raw meat to her in what is clearly a sexual gesture) this may well have been seen as more usual at the time the play was written. On the other hand, while it is possible to see him as fulfilling the stereotyped 'hunter-gatherer' male role of bringing the food back to his 'cave', to Blanche he really is 'practically a caveman' and she urges her sister 'not to hang back with the apes'. Moreover the sexual passion between Stanley and Stella is so strong that it makes it hard for the audience to see her as a passive victim of Stanley's violence in that she admits to being thrilled by it. When he smashed all the light-bulbs with her shoe on their wedding night, Stella interpreted this as evidence of his passion and she was prepared to surrender her old genteel life as a privileged Southern belle to be with him.

Stella and Stanley had met during the war, a time of immense social and cultural upheaval and dislocation when class barriers came down and anything seemed possible. Thus the arrival of Blanche, who is a direct reminder of Stella's aristocratic past at Belle Reve, is used by Williams to set the stage for a dramatic conflict between Stanley and Blanche which centres upon which one of them can exercise most influence over Stella. In fact they can't even agree on what to call her: Blanche refers to her romantically as 'Stella for star!' whereas Stanley's primitive yell of 'STELLAHHHHHH! is specifically likened in the stage directions to the noise of an animal. While the pet name 'honey' he uses for Stella may seem a little patronising, in fact other characters use this term too; in my opinion this is more a realistic feature of the New Orleans colloquial patois than evidence of casual sexism.

Blanche's dramatic function is to disrupt the status quo. When Stanley is on stage with Stella, he often has much longer speeches which suggest his dominance, but Blanche is a much more equal match for him. Williams's stage directions even colour-code their positions as protagonist and antagonist; whereas Blanche is like a 'moth' dressed in fluttering white, Stanley 'bounds into the room...wearing a red shirt'. His brilliantly coloured bowling shirt and gaudy striped silk pyjamas connote his physicality and energy. This quality in him means that when Blanche offers Stella sisterly support and Mitch the possibility of love, Stanley sees her invading his territory and threatening his dominant position as leader of the pack. The fact that she constantly hogs the bathroom suggests the battle lines have been drawn on stage, where the Kowalskis' apartment is quite literally not a big enough space for them both. Blanche's 'collapsible' camp-bed symbolises her temporary stay in Elysian Fields while the fact that there is only a flimsy curtain between her sleeping quarters and the rest of the apartment foreshadows Stanley's invasion of her personal space and that he will inevitably cross the line. Thus Williams offers the audience the possibility of viewing Blanche's tragic downfall as partly her own fault due to her 'enemy invasion' of Stanley's legitimate territory and her decision to contest his previously unquestioned dominance.

On the other hand Stanley is presented as more than just an extrovert, fun-loving, bumptious, working-class hero; much of his behaviour makes him seem downright devious and dangerous. What he suggests was merely protecting his old army buddy Mitch in revealing the truth about Blanche's past, is obviously an action also designed out of pure spite and malice and his birthday present of a bus ticket back to Laurel is unnecessarily cruel, showing his instinctive understanding of how to wound her most effectively. His Machiavellian nature is shown in Scene IV when he enters the apartment unknown to Stella and Blanche and eavesdrops on their heated conversation about him. Ominously he chooses to conceal himself and thus Williams makes use of intense dramatic irony in that the audience are uneasily aware of his presence whereas the two women continue to discuss him behind his back.

Stanley's astute ability to judge a situation and weigh things up to his own advantage is also shown when he notices Blanche's heavy drinking and unconvincing attempts to cover it up. Denying that she's been drinking his whisky Blanche declares, 'I rarely touch it.' Stanley mirrors her words by suggesting — with heavy irony — 'some people rarely touch it, but it touches them'. Later he insists on ripping down the Chinese paper lantern she has used to cover up the bright glare of a naked light-bulb in the apartment; Blanche quite rightly interprets this as another cruel attempt to expose and

humiliate her; Williams's stage directions state that '*Blanche cries out as if the lantern were herself*'.

Scene X is the play's dramatic climax. In many ways Stanley's rape of Blanche has been foreshadowed all along, for instance by his metaphorical violation of her trunk as far back as Scene II. Yet this apparently predestined outcome is challenged by aspects of Scene X which might be taken to suggest that Stanley did not set out with the intention of raping Blanche (and therefore breaking the incest taboo by proxy, in having sex with his sister-in-law). For instance the fact that the rape takes place 'off stage' might allow us to argue that it never took place at all, and was a figment of the insane Blanche's imagination; but Eunice's empathetic instruction to Stella — 'Don't ever believe it. Life has got to go on. No matter what happens, you've got to keep on going' — suggests that both she and Stella know instinctively that what Blanche had accused him of was true. Moreover Stanley's decision to set up a poker game for the day when Blanche is due to be taken to the asylum seems shocking and callous, and when even Steve and Pablo suggest Blanche's fate is 'bad' the audience is encouraged to disapprove of his actions along with his usually loyal cronies.

Top ten *quotation* ❯

On the other hand, his deviousness and cruelty can be offset with Blanche's snobbery, racism, dishonesty and manipulation. In Marxist terms, the working-class man is defending his hard-won economic, sexual and psychic territory from invasion by the forces of an oppressive aristocratic elite which wants to take back every scrap of capital he has scraped together to buy into the American Dream. Stanley does not wish to alter things but to preserve them the way they were before Blanche arrived in Elysian Fields, as he says to Stella: 'Stell, it's gonna be all right after she goes...You remember the way it was? Them nights we had together? God, honey, it's gonna be sweet when we can make them noises in the night the way we used to and get the coloured lights going with nobody's sister behind the curtain to hear us.' In a performance context, too, the iconic performance of Marlon Brando undoubtedly encouraged Williams's contemporary audience to identify with his character rather than that of the actress who originated the role of Blanche on the New York stage, Jessica Tandy, to the point where his defiant antagonism towards her often had the partisan audience clapping and cheering him on.

By the end of *A Streetcar Named Desire* Blanche has lost her pride, her culture and her sense of identity, but unlike a classical tragic hero she has obtained no insight into her condition — there is no anagnorisis, in terms of

Aristotelian dramatic theory. Thus on the whole I believe that Williams does not present Stanley as a Machiavel, but rather as an emblem for the new America. In my opinion the play cannot be divorced from its social, cultural and historical postwar context, and Tennessee Williams was realistic enough to present Blanche, who represents the moribund aristocracy of the Old South, as innately doomed from the outset as opposed to brought down by the external actions or machinations of an enemy antagonist such as Stanley, however powerful and cunning he might be.

Examiner's comments:

AO1 — quality of writing:

- an apt, clear and well written essay which creates and sustains an ongoing argument and achieves good cohesion across paragraphs
- aware of the possibility of a debate and alert to multiple meanings, which are signposted with appropriate discourse markers such as 'on the other hand', 'apparently' and 'thus on the whole I believe'
- demonstrates well-informed knowledge and understanding of literary techniques
- quotations are used effectively and adapted to the candidate's own required meaning

AO2 — form, structure and language:

- shows clear knowledge, understanding and analysis of relevant factors such as the genre of tragedy, dialogue, aspects of setting and stage directions

AO3 — comparison and interpretations:
(The first part of AO3 — comparison — is not assessed in this task)

- offers an interesting view of Stanley which recognises and celebrates the complexity of his characterisation and acknowledges the views of other readers and audiences

AO4 — context:

- covers a number of relevant social, cultural, historical, critical and performance contexts in some detail and weaves them into the overall argument. There are no 'bolted-on' sections of dubious relevance

Overall:

The student accesses all four AOs at a high level here and has done more than enough to earn a very good Grade A.

Extract-based (part-to-whole) tasks

Some tasks may require you to look at a specific section of the text in detail and then branch out from this to look at how and why key themes and ideas dealt with here may be reflected elsewhere in the play.

Key questions to ask when attempting any part-to-whole task:

- Why has Williams included this section and what is its place in the development of the plot?

- What is the function of the given section in the dramatic structure of the play — that is, how does this section fit into the play as a whole? Think about which previous scenes are recalled by this extract and/ or the extent to which it foreshadows future events. Are there any parallels or contrasts with other episodes? What would the play lose without this section?

- What does this section reveal about the major characters? Do we find out more information about existing characters and/or meet any new ones?

- How far might this section be seen as introducing, developing or illustrating one or more of the play's key themes, and how far is it typical of the ways in which Williams deals with these ideas elsewhere in the text?

- How far does the section illustrate typical aspects of Williams's form, structure and language? Does he use any recurring images or symbols, for instance? If so, analyse how they enhance the overall meaning of the text.

- What is the ratio or balance of stage directions to dialogue in the section? Is Williams using music or sound effects to evoke a particular mood, and if so, how does this work?

- What is going on between the characters present, and what is the impact of any entrances and exits? How is dialogue used to reveal character?

Sample task

> **Reread Scene IV. What impression is created of a) Blanche b) Stella and c) Stanley, and how far might the way in which they are represented here be seen as typical of their role in the play as a whole?**

The sample student essay which features in the 'Extended commentaries' section below models effective approaches to this sort of part-to-whole task.

Extended commentary

In all kinds of essay, you need to show that you can analyse form, structure and language in detail. It is well worth selecting a few key passages to analyse and set within the context of the whole text, as this type of task can help you to improve your writing skills as well as consolidate your knowledge and understanding of the play.

The extended commentary that follows was written by a Year 13 student who was allowed one hour of class time in which to complete the essay.

Sample task

> **Read from the stage direction *'During the pause...'* midway down page 8 of the Methuen edition to the stage direction *'Stanley, Steve and Mitch cross to the foot of the steps'* at the top of page 13.**
>
> **How does Williams use form, structure and language to present Blanche and Stella here and how does this section fit into the play as a whole?**

Sample answer

If the essence of drama is conflict, in this scene Williams uses the dynamic of the two sisters' relationship to advance the plot, introduce his key theme of the destructive nature of desire and establish the very different characters of Blanche and Stella. As they argue about the loss of their old plantation home, Belle Reve, the beautiful dream of their shared past, Williams gives Blanche naturalistic dialogue — 'I'm not meaning this in any reproachful way, but all the burden fell on my shoulders' — which is offset with those lyrical stage directions for a 'dimly lit' setting which evokes 'a mood for shadows from the past'. This may account for Williams's plays being referred to as 'dramatic poetry'.

At this point we have only just been introduced to Blanche, the febrile and flawed protagonist, and her younger sister, the down-to-earth Stella. Stella's obsession with her husband — whom the audience has already met, but Blanche has not — is clear as she talks of their mutual sexual passion, 'I can hardly stand it when he is away for a night...I cry like a baby in his lap.' When Blanche asks if Stanley will like her, Stella's unconvincing response that it will be 'fine' confirms the audience's own reading of this crucial relationship, based on what has been seen of him so far, hurling a package of raw meat

at Stella in a blatantly sexual gesture. Stella seems to know that there is bound to be trouble between Blanche and Stanley.

Stella's blind passion for her husband can be contrasted with her patient, tolerant resigned acceptance of Blanche's torrent of self-absorbed recriminations, 'a little wearily' she remarks 'It's just incredible, Blanche, how well you're looking.' By juxtaposing Stella's brief, clear lines with Blanche's outpourings and 'sharp laughs' Williams sets up a relationship which doesn't change for the rest of the play. Throughout the 11 episodic scenes of the play, which take place between early May and late October, Blanche's mental disturbance increases. At the heart of the play lies a web of sexual attraction, repulsion and repression which entraps both the sisters, and here death and desire are linked for the first time, as Blanche contrasts Stella's behaviour with her own. Stella abandoned the decaying house — 'Where were you...in bed with your — Polack' — while Blanche 'took the blows... You just came home in time for the funerals, Stella. And funerals are quiet, but deaths — not always.' Psychologically acute as always, early on in this memory play Williams shows Blanche driving Stella to tears by forcing her to recall what she would much rather forget. Blanche uses words as weapons here, and she knows how to hurt.

This scene is characteristic of Williams's 'plastic theatre' style in its use of vivid symbolism to add to the effect of the dialogue; the fact that 'there's no door between the two rooms' foreshadows that Stanley will inevitably cross the invisible dividing line between them, while Blanche's 'collapsible' bed suggests her presence in the Kowalskis' apartment will be only temporary. Later, as Blanche speaks, 'the music of the blue piano grows louder'. This ironic musical accompaniment embodies the lively jazz rhythms of the working-class multicultural Vieux Carré and undermines Blanche's evocation of the aristocratic past.

It seems that Blanche has always dominated Stella, who says, 'You never did give me a chance to say much...so I just got into the habit of being quiet around you.' Her patronising attitude to Stella, 'child you have spilt something on that pretty white lace collar of yours', shows Blanche's attempt to establish control over her sister perhaps to compensate for the fact that she has lost control over every other aspect of her life, while the stain on Stella's collar prefigures Blanche's hysterical reaction when she splashes coke on her own white dress and spoils it. This morbid sensitivity to stains and marks ties in with the obsessive bathing and obsessive ritual cleansing which will come to enrage Stanley.

With Stella's abandonment of Belle Reve, Williams invites the audience to assess the sisters' relative culpability; that is whether it was worse of Stella to leave, or of Blanche to stay. This foreshadows the play's denouement, when Blanche can no longer outrun her past and must finally submit to it, and Stella has to betray her sister in order to keep on living with Stanley. Williams suggests a fundamental similarity between the sisters here, in that just as Blanche's tragic flaw — the essential fault in her character which leads her towards inevitable destruction — is her helpless submission to desire, so this is Stella's weakness too.

You can find another extended commentary in the Downloads section of the free website at **www.philipallan.co.uk/literatureguidesonline**.

Top ten quotations

Look carefully at the following quotations and consider their significance within the play. How might they be used in an essay to help support your exploration of different elements or readings of *A Streetcar Named Desire*? Consider questions of form, structure and language, aspects of dramatic presentation, revelation of character, important themes and different critical interpretations of the text.

Ten 'top' quotations have been identified here, but you may well be able to suggest others which are equally significant in your opinion. Whichever you use, ensure that they are carefully integrated into your argument and not merely left hanging as little more than decorative essay-candy.

> BLANCHE: **They told me to take a street-car named Desire, and then transfer to one called Cemeteries and ride six blocks and get off at — Elysian Fields! (Scene I, p. 4)**

1

The central allegorical image of the play is this one of the streetcar which represents those forbidden sexual adventures which have brought Blanche to the land of the dead and represent the diametrically opposed Freudian impulses of *eros* and *thanatos*. Her sojourn at the Kowalskis' apartment will prove a sort of staging post in her journey towards that death-in-life in the asylum which is connoted by the end of the streetcar line — Cemeteries.

> BLANCHE: **...There are thousands of papers, stretching back over hundreds of years, affecting Belle Reve as, piece by**

2

piece, our improvident grandfathers and father and uncles and brothers exchanged the land for their epic fornications — to put it plainly!...The four-letter word deprived us of our plantation, till finally all that was left — and Stella can verify that! — was the house itself and about twenty acres of ground, including a graveyard, to which now all but Stella and I have retreated. (Scene II, p. 22)

Blanche's speech for the defence after Stanley accuses her of having cheated Stella lays the blame for the loss of Belle Reve squarely on their corrupt DuBois ancestors, but this only serves to stress that she is their direct heir in sexual as well as economic terms. Morally as well as financially bankrupt, Blanche represents the moribund Southern aristocracy who are utterly irrelevant in the new postwar world.

3

MITCH: Could it be — you and me, Blanche? (Scene VI, p. 57)

Mitch's touching proposal springs from the one time Blanche tells him the truth about her past and reveals the story of Allan Grey's suicide; his offer represents her last hope of finding someone to look after her. While she would never have seen the lumbering working-class Mitch as a suitable beau in her heyday, in her present circumstances Blanche recognises that he could offer her a lifeline. Ironically what causes him to abandon her may be her lies rather than her promiscuity, because when Stanley tells him about Blanche's past, Mitch feels she has made a fool of him.

4

STANLEY: I am not a Polack. People from Poland are Poles, not Polacks. But what I am is one hundred per cent American, born and raised in the greatest country on earth and proud as hell of it, so don't ever call me a Polack. (Scene VIII, p. 67)

As Blanche once again drops one of her unpleasant social clangers, Stanley attracts our sympathy, coming across as an all-American hero, forcefully (and rather magnificently) declaring that he is a son of Uncle Sam to his fingertips. The Old South she represents is dead in the water, while active, hardworking new Americans are popping up to claim their own piece of the American Dream.

5

STANLEY: When we first met, me and you, you thought I was common. How right you was, baby. I was common as dirt. You showed me the snapshot of the place with the columns. I pulled you down off them columns and how you loved it, having them coloured lights going! And wasn't we happy

together, wasn't it all okay till she showed here? (Scene
VIII, p. 68)

This quotation shows that, like Blanche, Stanley too has a public life and
a private inner life which is comprised of intimate memories, dreams and
desires. The coloured lights represent the passion between Stanley and
Stella which persuaded her to abandon her aristocratic past and build a
future with him in New Orleans. Unlike the cold white marble pillars of
Belle Reve, apparently the setting for a Greek tragedy, Stanley's 'coloured
lights' are vibrant and vivid. Whereas Blanche often wears white — this
is what her name means — Stanley wears gaudy bowling shirts and
bright silk pyjamas. This speech thus encapsulates Stella's dilemma,
caught between the past and the future.

STANLEY: **I've been on to you from the start! Not once did**
you pull any wool over this boy's eyes! You come in here
and sprinkle the place with powder and spray perfume and
cover the light-bulb with a paper lantern, and lo and behold
the place has turned into Egypt and you are the Queen
of the Nile! Sitting on your throne and swilling down my
liquor! I say — *Ha-Ha!* **Do you hear me?** *Ha-ha-ha!*
(Scene X, p. 79)

6

This is another of the play's frequent metatheatrical references to
acting and performance, as Stanley brutally strips away the pathetic
remnants of Blanche's dignity. Having previously referred to her putting
on 'her act' (p. 60), here he reveals his awareness of the gulf between
her constant masquerades and poses and the ugly truth beneath, and
mercilessly he brings her shaky house of cards tumbling down. Moreover
in mocking her as a dime-store Cleopatra, Stanley's speech also
foreshadows her eventual tragic downfall.

STANLEY: **We've had this date with each other from the**
beginning! (Scene X, p. 81)

7

Stanley's words here suggest that Blanche's fate has been decided all
along, and that the powerful sexual tension which has constantly arced
between them is about to short-circuit at the climax of the play. The
line jars slightly with what has come before it, as the dialogue between
Stanley and Blanche appears to allow for the possibility that they have
once again misunderstood one another, and that the rape was not in fact
premeditated; thus its inclusion surely suggests that Blanche's downfall
was inevitable, and all of a piece with Stanley's ominous remark to Stella
in Scene VII, 'Her future is mapped out for her' (p. 63).

8

EUNICE: Don't ever believe it. Life has got to go on. No matter what happens, you've got to keep on going. (Scene XI, p. 83)

Eunice's words to Stella encapsulate her working-class gut instinct for survival and authorise her friend's decision to abandon Blanche to her fate in order to go on living with Stanley. In the dog-eat-dog world of the new postwar America, Eunice knows that Stella has to put her love for her baby, her need for economic protection and the future of her marriage above her loyalty to her sister and her past, even if her feelings for Stanley are fatally compromised.

9

BLANCHE: ...I have always depended on the kindness of strangers. (Scene XI, p. 89)

Blanche's final words show that she has finally abandoned the real world for her fantasy life and reimagines the doctor who has come to take her to the asylum as the chivalrous beau (personified by Shep Huntleigh) by whom she longs to be rescued. Ironically it was her constant search for love and support — 'the kindness of strangers' — which led her to her ruin in the first place, although she seems to have accepted that she has no one else to turn to now Stella has deserted her. Several 'strangers' appear to Blanche during the play — the Young Man, the Mexican Woman, the Negro Woman and the Prostitute — and each encounter seems to leave her more isolated and vulnerable than the last.

10

STEVE: This game is seven-card stud. (Scene XI, p. 90)

As the men pick up the threads of their poker game after Blanche has been taken away to the asylum, Steve's words suggest that the game of life as played in the new America is one whose rules are laid down by — and serve to benefit — brutal men rather than vulnerable women. In this context, perhaps Stella's decision to stand by her man may seem the only sensible one she could make.

Taking it further

Books

- Bigsby, C. (2000) *Modern American Drama, 1945–2000*, Cambridge University Press
  - As well as being an excellent overview of twentieth-century drama which has much to say about other playwrights such as Arthur Miller, this book contains a very interesting chapter called

'Tennessee Williams: the Theatricalising Self'. Selected extracts from this book can be viewed online via a Google Books search.

- McEvoy, S. (2009) *Tragedy: A Student Handbook*, English and Media Centre
  - As well as being an excellent introduction to the tragic genre as a whole, this book contains a section on modern American tragedy which gives an overview of Williams's life and work and discusses *A Streetcar Named Desire*, *Cat on a Hot Tin Roof* and *The Glass Menagerie* in detail.

- Roudané, M. (ed.) (1997) *The Cambridge Companion to Tennessee Williams*, Cambridge University Press
  - A superb, thought-provoking collection of articles including Felicia Hardison Londré's 'A Streetcar Running Fifty Years'; Nancy M. Tischler's 'Romantic textures in Tennessee Williams's plays and short stories'; Gilbert Debusscher's 'Creative rewriting: European and American influences on the dramas of Tennessee Williams'; R. Barton Palmer's 'Hollywood in crisis'.

- Smith-Howard, A. and Heintzelman, G. (2005) *Critical Companion to Tennessee Williams: A literary reference to his life and work*, Checkmark Books
  - A Williams encyclopaedia, full of stimulating material.

- Williams, T. (ed. Margaret Bradham Thornton) (2006) *Notebooks*, Yale University Press
  - An intriguing scrapbook mix of diary, biography and autobiography.

- Williams, T. (1976) *Cat on a Hot Tin Roof and Other Plays*, Penguin
  - This collection includes Williams's fascinating essay 'Person-to-Person'.

- Williams, T. (1976) *Memoirs*, W. H. Allen
  - An absorbing patchwork autobiography covering many important aspects of Williams's life and work.

- Williams, T. (eds Patricia Hern and Michael Hooper) (1947) *A Streetcar Named Desire,* Methuen Student Edition 2008
  - An excellent edition of the text with a useful introduction and comprehensive glossary.

Internet

- Small. R. C. (2004) 'A Teacher's Guide to the Signet edition of Tennessee Williams's *A Streetcar Named Desire*' at: http://us.penguingroup.com/static/pdf/teachersguides/streetcar.pdf

- Robert C. Small's teachers' guide to the play is useful for students too, at: **www.turgingsomedrama.com/streetcar**
  - This website is built around a stage production at Indiana University of Pennsylvania. It features a host of interesting illustrations of many of the New Orleans landmarks mentioned in the play together with much other contextual information.

Films

- **1951:** directed by Elia Kazan — Tennessee Williams himself was closely associated with this film, the best-known interpretation, but it can be useful to look at other available versions too (as below) to see how and where their interpretations differ.
- **1984:** directed by John Erman — with Treat Williams as Stanley and Ann-Margret as Blanche.
- **1995:** directed by Glenn Jordan — with Alec Baldwin as Stanley and Jessica Lange as Blanche.